THE GINGERBREAD WITCH

BROOMSTICK BAKERY #3

LAURA GREENWOOD

Visit Laura Greenwood's website at:

www.authorlauragreenwood.co.uk

Cover by Ammonia Book Covers

The Gingerbread Witch is a work of fiction. Names, characters, places, and incidents are the products of the author's imagination or are used fictitiously. Any resemblance to actual persons, living or dead, business-es, companies, events, or locales is entirely coincidental.

If you find an error, you can report it via my website. Please note that my books are written in British English:

To keep up to date with new releases, sales, and other updates, you can join The Paranormal Council on Facebook or join my Mailing List via my website.

Contents

BLURB

Rowen wants to make certain that her time at the Christmas Fayre is well spent, especially when it comes to selling her magically infused cakes.

Edward loves the season, and jumps at the chance at helping his brother on the mulled wine stand.

When the two of them meet, sparks begin to fly and they realise that there might be something more between them than just a love of the fayre.

-

The Gingerbread Witch is a paranormal romance with a hint of Christmas spirit, a baking witch, and a light-hearted m/f romance. It is part of the Broomstick Bakery series.

CHAPTER 1

ROWEN

The bakery's sound system plays a cheery selection of Christmas music, and I find myself singing along even if I don't mean to. I don't normally care what's playing, but with the Christmas Fayre just days away, I know I need to get in the mood, not just so that my biscuits are infused with enough Christmas cheer to make anyone happy, but so that I'm ready to face the public.

Sadly, this is the one time of the year I can't ask any of my sisters to do it for me. I much prefer to manage things behind the scenes.

And bake. Always baking.

The kitchen door opens and I look up, surprised that any of them have shown up this early. We're not due to open for another couple of hours and as far as I know, they're all done with their prep.

"Hey, Rowen," my brother says, surprising me even more. I didn't expect him to be here.

"What's wrong?" I ask instantly.

He chuckles. "Why does anything have to be wrong?"

"You're nineteen and awake at six am," I point out. "It's fairly reasonable to assume there's something wrong." Especially as he's on holiday from the academy, so he can't even use class as an excuse.

"I was at Ellie's," he responds. "She got up for her internship, so I came here."

"They're working her harder than Granny used to work me," I joke.

"All I remember of that is that you were hardly ever home," he admits.

"That's because you were only ten at the time, you probably didn't care what your eighteen-year-old sister was doing."

"I care now."

"I'm not eighteen anymore," I point out. "You still haven't told me what the problem is."

"Because there isn't one," he says, coming further into the kitchens. "You're doing the Christmas Fayre this year, right?"

"Just like every year." Even if I don't like that I'm constantly having to deal with people there, I'd be a fool not to go, it earns far too much for the bakery and gets us new customers too. And I can never pass up an opportunity to help grow the bakery. We've worked too hard to make it into what it is today to let it slip through our fingers, and I know my sisters feel the same.

"You know how I helped you out on weekends last year?"

"Mmhmm. You want to get out of it this year?" I raise an eyebrow.

"What? No, of course not," he responds quickly, seemingly a little insulted by my insinuation. Guilt rushes through me. The last thing I want is to make my little brother feel bad.

"So, what is it?"

"I wanted to ask if you needed help on the other days too," he mumbles quickly. "I know the fayre can get busy and I thought you might like an extra hand."

"Oh." My surprise is evident in my voice and it's too late to hide it. "Are you short on money? I know Mum and Dad give you an allowance while you're at the academy, but I can help you out too."

He groans. "No, Row, I don't *need* extra money, I'm asking because I want to. I know it's important, I don't have any exams to prepare for, and Ellie has her internship at the moment. I'm at a loose end and I thought you might want some help." There's something in his voice that suggests there's another reason, but I doubt I'm going to get it out of him. I can't tell precisely what it is that he's being a little more secretive about, but it's something.

I push that to the side and choose not to worry about it. Knowing Ash, if he wants me to know what's bothering him, he'll tell me.

"Sure, you can come along if you want. It'll be nice to have company." It's a shame I can't send Ash on his own so I can help out here at the bakery. It won't just be busy for me at the fayre, but here for my sisters too, especially with Christmas just around the corner.

"Great. What do you need me to do?"

"You can box up the cupcakes Oakley made, they're in the trays over there." I gesture to them.

He heads to the sink to wash his hands and dons one of the Broomstick Bakery aprons. "What are they?"

"Mistletoe Kiss Cupcakes," I respond.

He raises an eyebrow. "And you said yes to those?"

I chuckle. "I'm not a dictator."

"That's what you think," he mutters under his breath.

I sigh. "She made a good argument about allowing them because they just felt like affection for the season. But we're not selling them to anyone under eighteen."

"That's going to be hard to get people to understand." He sets the first tray down on one of the benches and begins filling the cupcake boxes I've put there.

"That's what I said."

"And Oakley's response was..."

"To put a spiced rum jelly in the centre."

Ash lets out a rather justified laugh. I have to admit that I'm impressed with Oakley's method of dealing with the potential issue before it arises. And I do think that the cupcakes themselves are worth it. This isn't the first time she's made a cupcake infused with the emotions of a kiss, she's always been a hopeless romantic even before meeting Justin, and I'm starting to come around to the idea that they're not going to make people actually want to kiss, it's more about the feeling they get the moment *after* they've been kissed. The glow and the affection. Even if it's not something I personally want to experience from a cupcake, I can see why other people might.

Particularly those like Oakley who love everything about romance.

"What else are we taking this year?" Ash asks. "Some of Hazel's macarons, I assume?"

"We've got more of the Christmas Pudding ones, we always sell out. And she's made some that look like reindeer."

"She has?"

I nod. "The children's range of treats you suggested has been going down well," I admit, still impressed that he came up with it, especially when none of us did. "She thought they'd be a great addition to it for the Christmas period, so I said we'd test them at the fayre."

"They're going to do amazing."

"I think so," I agree.

"Your gingerbread normally do," he points out. "Because they're fun. Kids love fun."

"Have you been taking childcare lessons or something at the academy?"

He snorts. "Nope, not my thing." He closes one of the boxes and stacks it on top of the other full ones. "I'd rather learn about how to cook for a hundred guests." He looks over at me with a curious expression on his face, but I can't work out why.

We lapse into silence while I work on decorating my gingerbread and he packs up more of the cakes we need to take with us. It's comfortable to work with him like this, even with the ten-year age gap between us. I suppose it helps that the rest of our sisters are between us in age.

"Do these need loading into the van?" Ash asks, gesturing to the stacks of cupcake boxes.

I shake my head. "There's still all the stall stuff to go in, and I don't want to risk them freezing overnight, Oakley will never forgive us if her buttercream ends up crystallised." And more importantly, she doesn't have time to make more of them before the fayre starts.

"I'll sort the stall equipment," he says, already heading to the storeroom.

I watch him go and let out a relieved sigh. I wish I'd thought about asking him for help before, because it's going to be so much easier for me to manage everything the fayre entails with an extra pair of hands to help.

CHAPTER 2

ROWEN

Loud clangs and all kinds of shouts fill the air as the various stallholders at the Christmas Fayre set up for the days ahead. There's something nice about it, even if it's loud and chaotic. Perhaps it's because it's a reminder of the time of year and of the excited crowds to come.

I scan the stalls around me, unsurprised by the assortment. There are several local businesses in attendance, including a witch who makes knitwear charmed to shift with the owner, and the mead seller who I only ever see at these events and never anywhere else. Not that it'll stop me from buying from him, I always pick up a couple of bottles, particularly around Christmas time. Dad is a fan, and we all enjoy a tipple of mead after our Christmas dinner.

I push thoughts of purchasing mead to the side and focus on making sure my stall looks exactly the way I want it to, and that the banner displaying our logo is displayed in the best way possible.

I step back and look up at it, frowning at how off-centre the whole thing is. I let out a loud sigh. Back to square one with trying to put it up.

"Would you like a hand?" someone asks, making me jump.

I turn to find a tall blond man standing a few feet away.

"Sorry, I didn't mean to scare you."

"Then you shouldn't creep up on people," I retort.

He lets out a deep chuckle that's a surprisingly com-forting pitch. "I thought you knew I was there. I'm Edward." He holds out his hand.

I take it, eyeing him warily as I do. "Rowen." I like the way his hand feels around mine, strong and sure, but not like he's trying to overpower me with it.

"You're with Broomstick Bakery?" he asks, nodding to the sign.

I nod and let go of his hand. "And you are?"

"I'm at the mulled wine stand helping out my brother. Normally I'm a barrister."

"It's nice of you to help out," I murmur.

"Thanks. I love Christmas Fayres, there's something magical about them."

"There is," I agree.

"So, what does your bakery make?"

"Normal baked goods," I respond, confused that he hasn't heard of us. Most people in the area have.

"That's a cagey answer."

"I'm not under oath," I retort.

The corner of his lips lifts up into an amused smile. "That was a good one."

Pride fills me at his amusement. "I'm glad you thought so, but I'm afraid I don't have many more legal jokes in the wings."

"I have plenty, I can supply them if you supply the baking," he says with an easy smile. "Can I have a look?"

"You can, but everything is still boxed up. I don't want to get anything out until I've got the banner straight."

"You realise the fayre opens in half an hour?"

"Yes, that's why I was trying to get the banner up."

"Without help?"

"My sisters are back at the bakery dealing with the customers, and my brother will be here in about ten minutes." I'm not sure why I feel the need to explain myself to him, but I find myself doing it anyway.

"So that's a no."

I sigh. "I guess it is. But I can manage."

"I'm sure you can, but wouldn't you rather have some help?"

I bite my bottom lip, not wanting to admit anything when he seems so sure that he's worked out exactly who I am and what I need.

"I can help," he offers. "We're all set up anyway and I doubt anyone is going to want mulled wine at ten in the morning."

"Then you've clearly never worked a Christmas Fayre before."

"Correct," he responds. "This is the first time David's needed a hand."

I look up at the banner and assess my options, realising that it's probably going to take me the next half an hour to get the banner straight if I'm on my own, and while I may be exaggerating about the mulled wine, people do tend to want baked goods straight away.

"If you're willing, I'd appreciate the help," I say.

He flashes me a genuine smile. "Just tell me what to do."

"I need you to tell me whether it's straight," I say, making my way back up the step ladder and moving the banner slightly.

"You need to take it up a bit," he says. "No, too far, down a little. Right, there you go."

A small part of me is sceptical about his instructions, but I find myself tightening the ties anyway and returning to the ground. I take a few steps back and stare at my handiwork.

"Thank you," I tell Edward.

"You're welcome. It looks good."

"Thanks. If you come back once I'm all set up, I can give you a biscuit for your troubles."

He raises an eyebrow. "A biscuit?"

"Mmhmm, I make the gingerbread men myself and infuse them with Christmas cheer. Though if you'd prefer something else, I have Mistletoe Kiss cupcakes, Warm By The Fire brandy snaps, and Joyful Peppermint macarons."

"Are those just fun names?"

"Oh, no, we infuse our baking with emotions. It doesn't override anything that the consumer is feeling themselves, but it'll give them a warm feeling."

"And that's a real thing?"

"It is if you're a witch."

"If you're a witch, why didn't you use magic to hang the banner?" He looks up at it.

"Some things are better done by hand," I respond.

He chuckles. "You're not wrong there. Once I tried to tie my shoelaces with magic. That didn't end well."

"You're a warlock?" I ask.

"Unless my parents have something important to tell me and a lot of explaining to do."

"Then why did you ask why I put the banner up by hand? Surely you knew the answer?"

"Perhaps I just like asking questions. It's what I'm paid to do." There's a twinkle in his eyes as he says it, suggesting that he might be teasing me.

"Not here, it isn't."

"Asking people how many mugs of mulled wine they want is a question."

"You're enjoying yourself far too much," I say.

"Am I not supposed to be? I thought the Christmas Fayre was supposed to be about having fun and enjoying the season?"

"Maybe for you, and for the visitors, but this is an important part of my business calendar. Doing well here means that we'll have more customers for the bakery all year around. It's no laughing matter."

He raises an eyebrow. "You're the oldest, aren't you?"

"What?"

"Of your siblings. You mentioned sisters and a brother. You're the eldest, right?"

"Yes. But I'm not sure what that matters."

He shrugs. "I suppose it doesn't."

I narrow my eyes at him, trying to work out what he's trying to achieve by being this way. "I need to get back to work," I murmur.

"Then I'll let you get to it," he responds. "But I'll be back later for my Christmas Cheer gingerbread man. I must admit to being intrigued by the concept." And from his voice, he sounds like he's sceptical about whether it'll actually make him feel the emotion I'm promising.

I'm not phased by it. Edward-the-mulled-wine-seller's-brother isn't the first person to doubt the effects of our cakes, and he isn't going to be the last either. Everyone converts once they've had a taste and realised that they do exactly what we say they do.

He'll be no different.

"Thanks for your help," I say, remaining polite despite his attempts to infuriate me.

"See you in a bit," he responds, waving and heading back in the direction of the mulled wine stand.

I remain in position for a few moments, trying to work out precisely what just happened and why the interaction bothers me so much, because I doubt it's about having to give away a gingerbread man for free, or not being able to sort out the banner by myself.

I shake my head to rid myself of any lingering thoughts about the interaction. I need to focus my attention on making sure all of the cakes are in the right places. At least Ash should be here momentarily and I won't have to do the first rush myself. I'm glad he asked to work the fayre more this year, I think I'm going to need all of the help I can get.

I glance in the direction of the mulled wine stand, but I can't see anything from this far away. Sometimes, help comes from the most unexpected of places.

CHAPTER 3

EDWARD

I hand over three mugs of mulled wine and take payment from the customers, only half surprised to discover that Rowen was right about how early people want alcohol while visiting a fayre like this. It doesn't seem to be acceptable any other season of the year, but when Christmas is involved, day drinking seems to not just be accepted, but encouraged.

I can't imagine it will end well for some people.

A woman walks past with a Broomstick Bakery tote bag that seems to be bursting at the seams with baked goods, and I find my mind straying back to the promise of getting to try one of the witch's creations. I'm not sure I believe that it'll make me feel anything more than any other well baked gingerbread biscuit would, but I'm willing to be proved wrong.

"What do you know about Broomstick Bakery?" I ask my brother.

Surprise flits across his face at my question, which I suppose is fair, I haven't shown any previous interest in what any of the other stalls are selling.

"It's a bakery across town," David responds despite his confusion. "I think they're over at stall sixty-seven. Why?"

I consider brushing off the question, but decide it's better not to. "I met the owner earlier, she invited me to go and try one of her biscuits."

"Then you should," he responds. "They're good. Freddie often stops by there on the way home from work to get us something." A loving smile spreads over his face at the mention of his husband.

"Mind if I go now?" I ask. "We're not busy."

"Go for it. But come back if you see a stampede of people heading for me."

I chuckle. "That seems unlikely, even if we've been busier than I expected. Want me to pick anything up for you to take back to Freddie?"

"Oh, yes. That'll be nice. I don't think he'll be able to stop there on the way back tonight. It'll be nice to surprise him."

"What do you want?" I ask.

"Hmm. Good question. Whatever is good."

"I think she said they have some Mistletoe Kiss cupcakes, whatever they are."

David's eyes light up. "They sound perfect. Get me two of those, please."

"You got it." I pat my pocket to check I've got my phone and my wand and head out from behind the stall and back down to the stall in question, trying to ignore how excited I feel to be heading back to see Rowen. I barely know her, and she didn't seem particularly impressed with me earlier, which means I shouldn't feel like this.

And yet I do. Maybe it's because she didn't seem in the slightest bit intimidated by my job title, which is a rarity in itself.

A dark-haired guy that looks a little like her but younger deals with a customer. That must be the brother she mentioned, but there's no sign of Rowen.

"Ah, you came back."

I turn around to find the witch in question standing behind me with an amused smile on her face. Her auburn hair is pulled back from her face in a neat low bun, and she's now wearing a pale blue apron with the bakery's logo on over her jeans and jumper. It's nothing fancy, but she looks good.

"How could I say no to the promise of ginger-bread?"

"Are you a particular fan?" she asks, gesturing to me to follow her towards the counter.

"I haven't had any in years," I admit. "But I used to make it all the time with my Grandma. It brings back happy memories."

"Then I'm happy we can help you with that."

"Is that why you set up the bakery?" I ask. "To help people relive childhood memories?"

"We didn't found it," she responds. "It's a family business going back generations, we're just the current custodians."

I raise an eyebrow. "And all of your siblings are involved?"

"My sisters, yes. Ash just does some odd jobs now and then for us." She nods towards her brother who tenses when she says it.

It seems that he's not a fan of being thought of that way. Or perhaps I'm reading into the situation too much. It wouldn't be the first time I've done it, though I should be more careful of getting carried away. Not everyone wants to be analysed as to their motives.

"So, which gingerbread man do you want? We have Santa, a snowman, Rudolph, or just the traditional version," she says, gesturing to each in turn.

"Wouldn't Rudolph be a ginger-reindeer not a gingerbread man?" I ask.

"Technically, yes, but it's easier to just print off one ticket," she responds. "Is Rudolph the one you want?"

"That depends."

"On?"

"Which you're the proudest of."

"They're all the same recipe," she says.

"Which doesn't mean anything. Perhaps one of them baked longer, or you're particularly proud of the detail you put in the decoration of one." It's always the little things that elicit the most pride, in my experience.

"The classic," she admits, picking one from the back with tongs and placing it in a bag for me. "I know I'm supposed to say one of the fancier ones, but I'm too traditional for that."

"Then why make the others?"

"Because as my siblings like to point out, I can't do everything my way if I want to stay in business, and other people like the fun shapes."

"Well, I'm a fan of tradition," I admit.

A small smile pulls at the corners of her lips. "Why am I not surprised?"

"I did just ask for a traditional gingerbread man instead of anything fancy," I point out.

"Under the guise of picking the one I was proudest of." She holds the bag out to me.

I reach out to take it from her, our fingers accidentally brushing against one another as I take it.

Her breathing hitches at the contact, and I linger for a moment longer than is totally necessary.

She doesn't pull away either, something that doesn't go unnoticed.

Rowen clears her throat and let's go. "I hope you enjoy." Her voice slips into her customer tone, which I find I hate more than I should.

"Do you mind if I eat it here?" I ask.

Her eyebrow raises. "Sure, if you want. Most people take it away with them."

"But then I'll have to come back if I want more," I point out. "Oh, though my brother did want me to pick him up two of those Mistletoe cupcakes if you still have some."

She nods and moves down the stall to wear a row of cupcakes topped with glittering sugar paste mistletoe sit. I'm not a fan of cupcakes, but even I have to admit that they look good.

I stare at her for a moment before realising how rude I'm being and tearing my gaze away. I don't want to make her uncomfortable, especially when she's busy sorting out cakes for my brother.

Needing something to do with my hands, I unwrap the gingerbread man and pull it out of the packet. Even from my limited experience with them, I can tell it's a good one, and the scent of the spices fills my nose.

It's a little weird to bite into it, and I find myself transported back years to when I was a child. Maybe this is what she means when she says the biscuits are full of Christmas Cheer. It's not that they're full of actual emotion, but that they remind people so well of the past.

The biscuit tastes as good as it smells and I take another bite just as the previous one hits my stomach. Warmth spreads through me, followed by a swell of sentiment towards the season and the joy it brings. My whole body tingles as it spreads through me. I'm still aware of my own surprise and curiosity beneath the way the biscuit has made me feel, but there's definitely something there.

My gaze latches on to an amused-looking Rowen standing in front of me with a box of cupcakes in her hands. "Believe me now?" she holds them out to me.

"I do." I take them from her. "How much do I owe you?"

"They're on the house."

"Are you sure?"

Amusement dances through her eyes. "Your face when you ate the gingerbread was payment enough."

"Hey, Rowen?" her brother calls.

"I have to go," she says. "Enjoy the rest of it."

She heads away before I can answer, but it doesn't matter. I can say with certainty that this isn't the last time I'm going to see the enchanting baker.

CHAPTER 4

ROWEN

My feet ache, and if I think about it, so does my back. I love the fayre, but it always takes such a toll on my body, and this year is going to be worse than normal if it keeps being as busy as this.

"That'll be eleven pounds sixty, please," I say to the vaguely familiar woman in front of me.

"Card, please," she responds.

"All right." I pick up the machine and input the numbers, wondering why no one has come up with a card reader that automatically recalls the amount spoken aloud. Magic is supposed to be good for making business easier, but sometimes, I don't think that's true. "Here you go." I hold out the machine to her.

She taps her card and waits for the beep. "Thanks. By the way, I got some of your new animal cupcakes for my grandkids last week. They absolutely loved them, said they were the best ones they've ever had from the shop."

"I'll make sure to let my sister know, she'll be thankful to hear it," I respond with a genuine smile. Oakley works hard to make sure she's always coming up with good flavours, decorations, and emotions for her cupcakes. I know she'll like hearing that her efforts have been appreciated.

"It's the whole bakery," she responds. "They keep nattering me about getting them more cakes ever since you brought in your children's range. They love it, even if my bank account doesn't. Still, it's worth it." She smiles widely.

I return the gesture, knowing she means exactly what she's saying. There's always an earnestness to people that's easy to spot when they talk about good food.

"Right, I'd best be off. Enjoy your day," she says.

"You too." I wave her off.

"Who was that?" Ash asks, the somewhat smug expression on his face revealing that he heard the entire conversation. And it's warranted. The children's range was his idea, and it's been doing great for the bakery. Which reminds me that I need to talk to the others about giving Ash some kind of bonus over it all. He doesn't get a share of the bakery's normal proceeds, so only gets paid when he works, and I want to make sure he knows how much we value him suggesting things that make the business stronger.

"I'm not sure," I admit. "But she sounds like a regular customer. Sometimes, I wonder if it would be better if Clover came to these things instead of me. She knows the regulars so much better." Mostly because I avoid them.

"But if Clover was the one here, then she'd be the one making eyes at the mulled wine stand every chance she got," he jokes.

"I am not making eyes at anyone."

"Sure, sure."

"You should respect your elders, Ash."

He snorts. "You're my sister, that gives me a pass."

"Hmm. I'm also your boss right now," I say. "Though it's nearly clocking off time. What have we got left?"

"Not much, but most of it we have more of back at the bakery, or would be made fresh tomorrow morning anyway," he responds, instantly slipping into business mode. It's impressive how good he is at that.

"Most isn't all," I point out.

"We're nearly out of the Christmas Pudding macarons."

"Already?" I can't keep the surprise out of my voice. "Hazel already made more than last year."

"Maybe there are more in the van still?" he suggests, though I can tell from his tone that he doesn't think there are. Either he's checked, or he's keeping better track of the stock than I am, which is a little embarrassing for me, but is good for him. "I can check."

"No need, I believe you. I'll message her and ask her to make more. There should be enough time before tomorrow so long as she doesn't have a cooking class to teach this evening."

"Aren't they closed for the holidays?" he asks. "I'm pretty sure she said something about Antonio using the time to do some dish development."

"Did she?" I grimace. I should pay more attention. Now Ash is telling me all of this, I have to admit that it does sound vaguely familiar. My head has just been too full of preparations for the fayre and the general running of the business over the Christmas season. Sometimes, I wish I was capable of asking one of my sisters to do more. It's not even that I can't trust them to do it, I know all three of them would be more than capable, it's that I don't feel properly able to let go. I need to have the control.

"She did," Ash responds, pulling me back to the conversation. "But I'm sure she'll be bringing him in to help with the macarons."

"He'll do anything if he can spend time with her."

"I suspect the fact he's the son of one of the most famous patissiers in the world probably helps with how chill you are about that," Ash responds.

I shrug. "Normally, it wouldn't be great, especially with the added cost of paying him, but we're only a day into the fayre, we need those macarons, so I'll okay whatever price Antonio sets for his time."

"I'm going to tell him you said that," Ash jokes.

"Even if you do, it's fine." Hazel's boyfriend is well aware of his worth, he'll demand the amount he deserves from the bakery books, and it'll be worth it for the extra macarons Hazel will be able to make while she has a sous-chef as talented as him.

Just like I'll happily let Oakley's boyfriend help with advertising on social media. I hate it, he's good at it, as far as I'm concerned, it's fine so long as I pay him.

"Want me to start clearing down?" Ash asks.

I nod. "But start with the stuff no one can see and we'll do the cakes last. There are still some stragglers, and you know what the stall holders are like. They won't have had time to visit earlier, so they'll do it now."

"Stall holders in general, or just one in particular?" Ash wiggles his eyebrows.

I groan. "I preferred it when you were five and didn't understand any of this." Especially because there's a part of me that knows he's right. Despite knowing it's pointless, and that it would never lead to anything, there's a part of me that's hoping Edward will pop back so I have an excuse to talk to him again.

"I was also more likely to eat the cakes than sell them then."

"Remember that time you did? Granny was fuming." I'd only been sixteen or so and had been helping her like Ash was helping me now. Mum had left Ash with us for the afternoon, and we went back into the bakery kitchen to find him in a daze after eating a dozen cupcakes.

"I felt sick after that."

"So you should have, it was a lot to eat, especially for a six-year-old."

"I never did it again, though," he points out.

"Want to know a secret?" I ask.

"Is it about how you're crushing on the mulled wine vendor?" he teases.

"I'm twenty-nine, I don't have crushes."

"Are you sure?" He smirks as if he knows how much I'm lying. "But sure, what secret?"

"Maybe I won't tell you after all."

"Are you sure you're twenty-nine?"

I let out an amused laugh. "You've gotten cheeky in your old age."

"I've always been cheeky," he counters. "The secret?"

"Right, well when I was seven, I did exactly the same and ate through Granny's entire basket of brandy snaps. I threw up all over the bakery floor."

He wrinkles his nose at the visual. "I didn't know that."

"I'm not surprised, I kept it almost as quiet as Hazel did the time she got into the buttercream, or when Clover and Oakley ate an entire bucket of popping sprinkles and ended up doing jumping jacks all around the house for three days." I smile at the memories.

"I think I remember the twins doing that."

"They were quite memorable," I agree. "But we all overindulged at some point."

"Maybe Granny did too."

"I'm sure she did, though I find it hard to imagine." She's a woman full of love, but she can be quite stern at times, imagining her gorging herself on sweet treats to the point of sickness is somewhat difficult. "Right, we should pack up. I'm sure you want to get back to see Ellie, and I'm dying for a bubble bath and a cup of hot chocolate. You can even go now if you want, I can deal with it."

"She's not off work yet," he assures me. "I can help with the clear down."

"Thanks, Ash, I really appreciate it."

"You are paying me," he points out.

"Even so, I'm grateful."

He smiles in response and turns his attention to packing up the various pieces of equipment that need to go back to the bakery so they can go through the dishwasher. I pull out my phone and send a quick message to Hazel to make sure she gets started on the macarons before helping him.

It's hard to believe that I was planning on doing all of this on my own, but I'm very glad that I'm not.

I look over my shoulder in the direction of the mulled wine stand, trying to ignore the disappointment over Edward not having come over at the end of the day.

I shake my head to rid myself of the thoughts. We've had two conversations, and while he seems like a decent guy, that's just not enough to base anything on. I should put him from my mind and focus on what I'm supposed to be doing instead, even if there's a part of me that doesn't want to.

CHAPTER 5

ROWEN

I wrap my hands around the steaming mug of hot chocolate in front of me and let out a loud sigh. Three days of working the fayre have already left me feeling stiffer than normal, and even with the heat pouring off the multiple ovens in the bakery kitchen, I can still feel the cold from an entire day in the outside air deep within me.

"Is this seat taken?" Oakley asks.

I look up and smile at my sister. "Be my guest." I gesture for her to sit.

She puts her own mug down on the table and slides in opposite me.

"What's up?" I ask.

"Nothing, you just look like you need company."

I consider arguing with her, but I think it's safe to say that she knows me better than that.

"Sales are good," she says. "Ash's children's range is doing well. We should make sure to do something for him for that, I don't want him to think that we're just going to steal his ideas."

"I was thinking of a bonus," I respond.

"Sure."

I narrow my eyes. "You don't agree? Shouldn't he be paid for his ideas?"

"Yes, of course. Especially those that make the bakery better."

"But?" I prompt.

"But is it enough?"

I frown. "What do you mean?"

"Seriously, Row, for someone so smart, you can be really dumb sometimes."

"I take offence at that."

"You don't even know why I'm calling you dumb." She takes a sip of her coffee.

"You're going to enlighten me, aren't you?" I can tell from the tone in her voice. Her twin is exactly the same. I don't know how Mum and Dad coped with all of us at once.

"Look, Ash is clearly interested in more than just the odd job here and there. Maybe it's time we offer him something more than that."

I blink a few times as I try to process what she's suggesting. "More than that?"

"Yes. I mean, with his studies, he can't take on a full share of bakery duties, but maybe in the future..."

"I don't think Ash is even interested in the bakery."

She gives me an incredulous look. "Then you should start paying more attention."

Surprise flits through me, both at her observation, and the fact she's being so stern with me. Oakley is easily the softest of the five of us when it comes to these kinds of things. Maybe she's redirected some of her romantic dreaming now she's found Justin.

"I will do," I promise.

"Good. How are you doing at the fayre? Hazel said she's already had to make more macarons, that sounds promising."

I nod. "I think the idea to not sell them at the bakery until the fayre is over is helping there."

"Mmm, I've had a lot of people asking for them today."

A frown pulls at my forehead. "Today?"

"Yes, as in the day that just happened. Why? Should we not have?"

"I thought Clover was working the front?"

"She was, but you know what December is like for sales, we're all needed."

"Right, sorry. I forgot."

Oakley shrugs. "It's fine, you don't spend much time at the shop this time of year."

"That sounds really bad."

"Maybe, but we all know what you're doing is important. Our Christmas orders are through the roof this year."

"Already?" That's surprising, there are still a few weeks left of the fayre, I didn't expect my efforts to start making a difference for another week or so.

Well, our efforts. Even if Oakley is wrong about Ash, he's still doing a lot for the bakery at the fayre, and he never slacks.

"I'm guessing all the effort you put into the fayre in the past few years is paying off," she points out. "And Justin started some adverts for us, they're probably bringing people in."

"I must admit, it's useful to have your boyfriend around."

"Yes, usefulness to my family is precisely why I decided to date Justin." She shakes her head in bemusement.

"How's it going? Still in newly-moved-in-bliss?"

"Don't you know it." She lets out a wistful sigh.

"How did you know?"

"Know what?" She takes another drink.

"That Justin was right for you."

She shrugs. "I guess I just did. But it's not as simple as that. Sure, there was a connection, it didn't spring out of nowhere, but it still takes work. We decide that we love each other every day."

"And that's worth it?"

"Of course. I may be a romantic, but I'm also pragmatic."

An involuntary snort escapes me. "Sorry," I mutter.

"I'm serious," Oakley responds. "I know that our relationship won't just take care of itself, I have to put the time in, and so does Justin. That's what makes it work."

"Does he do anything that annoys you?"

An amused smile stretches over her face. "He's terrible at putting his socks in the wash basket."

"That's it?"

"There have been other things, just like there are things he finds annoying about me. But we either talk about it or fight about it, and then we deal with it and move on."

"Huh." I lean back in my seat. "That seems like an effort."

"You've never been in love, have you?" she asks. "Not even Mickey?"

"I don't think so," I respond. "But how would I know?"

"I think you'd know if you loved someone. You dated Mickey for years, did you seriously never tell him that you loved him?"

"Yes, I told him."

"But you don't think you were?"

"I think I believed I was. But I'm not sure. It hurt when he ended things to move to America, but I don't think it hurt as much as it should." Even now, there's a small pang of regret that things didn't work out with my only long-term boyfriend, but it's nothing more than that. There's no pain or hurt. He did what was right for him at the time.

"Hmmm."

"What?"

"Nothing," Oakley mutters.

"Oak," I say sternly.

"I find it interesting that you're asking about this now."

"You and Hazel have recently gotten into relationships, and Clover hasn't properly been single in about ten years."

Oakley snorts. "Clover is completely single, she has the occasional fling, she just doesn't tell us when they end."

"Is she seeing someone at the moment? Is that where she's sneaking off to all the time?"

"It's not sneaking if she leaves through the front door and tells us where she's going," she points out. "Besides, she's twenty-seven, I don't think that counts as sneaking anyway."

"So where's she going?"

"The coffee shop."

"Huh, she's spending a lot of time there."

"She and Willow have been close for years," Oakley reminds her. "And they've gotten closer since everything with Azíl happened and Willow needed more help."

"And that doesn't bother you?"

"Why would it? Because we're twins and supposed to be inseparable? You know we've never been like that unless there's mischief involved. We have our own lives."

I should know this, and I suppose I do. While it's easy to think of them as twins sometimes, I'm well aware that they're completely different people, with different skill sets and desires in life.

The bell in the shop rings and her whole face lights up.

"Is it not locked?" I ask.

"It is, but we changed the spells so Justin could come in now it's cold," she reminds me. "I'll see you tomorrow. I'm coming in early to make a new batch of cupcakes for you, Ash had an idea about some reindeer ones."

"Don't you think reindeer macarons are enough? And gingerbread. We don't need everything in reindeer."

"It's a Christmas Fayre, Row. The opposite is true. Everything should be reindeer." She gets to her feet and takes her mug over to the dishwasher, setting it down to go through the machine when we turn it on tomorrow. "Don't stay up too late."

I chuckle. "I'm heading to bed in a minute," I promise, more than a little amused that she's the one telling me what to do when I'm older than she is.

"See you tomorrow, Row." She waves and heads through to the main shop. The low rumble of a man's voice greets her, confirming what she already assumed to be true about Justin waiting for her.

Despite knowing that our paths in life are different, I can't help the small flare of jealousy that bursts to life inside me. I've never wanted the same things as Oakley, or as my other sisters, but apparently, seeing her happy and in love is enough to make it spring to life. And the desire to have someone of my own around to support me is almost overwhelming.

An image of Edward from the mulled wine stand smiling at me springs into my mind.

My eyes widen and I squash it down. It's nothing more than a silly crush like the ones I had in school, it'll go away. It has to, because the last thing I have time for is feeling like this. Or romance in general.

I have a bakery to run, a Christmas Fayre to sell at, and a whole host of other things to achieve. I'm not going to let some errant thoughts of a near stranger ruin any of that.

CHAPTER 6

ROWEN

Despite the chill hanging in the air as the sky gets darker, I'm still warm from the exertions of running around constantly. Despite how small our stall is, there's a lot of moving about, especially as we're constantly needing to restock.

"I swear we're going to need a third person on Saturday," I mutter.

Ash chuckles. "Think Willow can spare Azíl for the day? He'd love this."

"He'd eat all the cake," I retort, unable to suppress the wave of affection that spreads through me at the thought of our cousin's boyfriend. I thought it was weird at first that she fell for a three-thousand-year-old warlock she found cursed to live in a teapot, but as I've gotten to know him, I've come to appreciate how it might have happened.

Helped along by just how much he loves our cakes, naturally.

"He'd still help. Everyone loves him at Cauldron Coffee," Ash responds. "And he works hard."

Right, Clover isn't my only sibling who has done some shifts for Willow recently. Ash has been working there too. Which should have made me realise him asking to help at the fayre was nothing to do with money. He should have plenty of it between what we pay him, and what Willow is bound to have.

"It's a good idea, but it's a Saturday, I'm sure Willow will need him at the coffee shop." I imagine a lot of the fayre visitors will stop there on the way back in an attempt to warm themselves up.

"Ah, right. I could ask Ellie? I know she isn't famil y..."

"She's as much family as Azíl is," I point out. "Do you think she'd be okay to help? She must be tired from her internship."

"She is," he admits. "But she's also got more energy than I think I've ever seen her have before."

"That happens when you follow your passion."

"Yes," he agrees quietly.

"If you think she'll be okay to help, then yes, please. Obviously we'll pay her. Actual money and cake."

He snorts. "That's probably more than she's getting paid at the moment."

"Sad, but true." I remember the pay from my own internship. It was truly atrocious.

Ash clears his throat. "I'll ask. You've got company by the way." He nods to the left.

I frown and turn in time to see Edward approach with a cup holder.

My heart skips a beat, and as much as I hate to admit it, even to myself, there's been a part of me hoping he'd come over for the entire day.

"Hey," he says.

"Hi." My voice comes out small and squeaky.

Ash laughs softly behind me, but I ignore him. He's just being an annoying little brother, and I know the best way to deal with that is to ignore it.

"I wanted to come by yesterday, but we had a surge of customers at the end of the day," Edward says.

"That'll happen when you're selling hot drinks on a cold day."

"Mmm, true. But I thought I'd bring you some mulled wine. You let me try what you make, so I thought I'd return the favour. Though as far as I'm aware, it won't do anything other than taste good." He smiles and holds out the tray to me. "I brought one for your brother too."

I stare at him, unable to process what's happening, though I'm not entirely sure why.

"Thanks," Ash says, picking up one of the cups. "I haven't had time to get anything from any of the other stalls yet." He nudges me gently with his elbow.

"Thank you," I say, finally finding my words. "It's very thoughtful of you." I pick up one of the takeaway cups, the warmth spreading through it to my fingers in a delightful way.

"Maybe I just want to get another gingerbread man from you," he says with a grin, taking the third cup for himself.

"We've sold out, I'm afraid."

"But I'll put one aside for you tomorrow," Ash pipes up.

I glare at my brother.

"So I haven't had a chance to look around the fayre yet," Edward says. "And I realised you probably haven't either, so wanted to know if you would join me?"

"I..." Should I say yes? There's a large part of me that wants to. Even if I don't know Edward very well, I have to admit to enjoying his company during the brief conversations we've had. But I'm needed here.

"I'll be fine," Ash says. "You should go."

I nod. Only half annoyed at his interference.

Edward's face lights up. "Great." He steps back and waits for me to join him.

I glance at the stall, trying not to let the guilt over leaving Ash alone overtake me. He knows what he's doing, and his knowledge of the products we have on sale is great. Which is probably one of the reasons

Oakley thinks he might be interested in being more than an occasional helper at the bakery.

I fall into step beside Edward, unsure precisely what we're doing, other than looking around the fayre. Is this supposed to be a friendly even, or are we trying to be date-like?

Desperately needing a distraction, I take a sip of my drink, the tartness of the wine explodes on my tongue, followed by the warmth of the spices. "This is good," I say, lifting the hand holding my cup so he knows what I'm talking about.

"It is," he agrees. "We make the wine ourselves."

I raise an eyebrow. "I thought you were a barrister?"

"I am."

"But you also make wine?"

"Is that so hard to believe?"

"It just seems unlikely," I admit.

"Are you saying that you've always worked at your family bakery? You've never had another job?"

"I haven't," I admit. "But my other siblings have."

"Even Ash? He looks like he's still at school."

I let out a soft snort. "He's in his second year at Grimalkin."

"That's quite an age gap."

"I don't know if that's an insult or not."

"Oh, erm, yes, that sounded bad. I was just guessing. You're the eldest sibling, you mentioned multiple sisters, so I'm assuming he's the youngest. Which would put you at twenty-five?"

"Nice save." Amusement shines through my voice. "There's a ten-year gap between me and Ash, and six years between him and my youngest sister."

"Ah, so he really is the baby of the family."

"Something like that. It's hard to remember he's an adult now, even if I know it's true."

"I can imagine. Well, I can't. I only have one brother, and there are only eighteen months between us. I can't imagine what it's like to have three siblings."

"Four," I correct.

"Wow, your parents must have had their hands full."

I let out an amused laugh. "Including twins."

"Twin witches? That sounds like a nightmare."

"*Identical* twin witches."

"I dread to think about the mischief they got up to," he responds.

"They weren't so bad," I admit, a smile rising to my face while talking of my sisters. "But you never explained about the winemaking. Is it a hobby? No, you asked about my family business when I mentioned it, so it's that?"

"Good deductive skills," he says. "It's a family vineyard. David works there alongside our Dad."

"But you decided to become a barrister instead?"

He shrugs. "The law has always interested me. And I didn't inherit Dad's green fingers. He's a dryad, but you know how genetics work."

"Not in great detail," I admit.

"Well, witch DNA comes out on top when paired with dryads, meaning both David and I are warlocks. But my brother still has an affinity for plants despite that."

"Sometimes, the blood just can't be overwritten," I say.

"Precisely. Oh, look, they have handmade ornaments. I should get one for Mum, she'll love it. Mind if we take a look?" He stops walking while waiting for my response, and I do the same.

"Be my guest, I'm sure mine would like one too."

"Before we do, there's actually something I meant to ask you," he says, not making a move towards the stall.

"Oh?"

"Would you like to go on a proper date with me? One that doesn't involve a thinly veiled excuse of walking around a fayre."

I chuckle. "Is that what that was?"

"Guilty as charged."

"Barrister joke?"

"You know it." He grins. "So, a proper date?"

"Yes." The word slips out before I mean it to. "A proper date sounds great."

And I actually mean it, even if I think it's foolish to feel this way about someone I've just met. But I suppose everyone has to meet somehow, and this is just the way the two of us have. I shouldn't dismiss whatever this is just because of the circumstances, especially when I like his company.

So I'm going to take a chance and see where this goes, even if it feels rather contrary to my usual approach.

Chapter 7

Edward

I don't think I've ever been this nervous about a date before. Nor have I been this sure. Every other time I've considered starting something with someone, there's been weeks of dancing around one another and light flirting.

And yet with Rowen, there have been days. And for most of that time, we've been in separate stalls doing our own thing and kept busy by the guests of the fayre. But there's something about the way she makes me feel that can't fully be explained other than using the word *right*. It's almost as if the warm fuzzy feeling I got from eating her gingerbread man comes from her as well as the biscuit. Though I know that isn't possible, not when the effects aren't made to last anyway, nor is it possible for them to replace real emotion. It's a fascinating branch of magic that I don't know much about but spent some time reading up on once I experienced it.

The bakery is still lit up and there are several customers inside when I arrive, and I worry that I got the time wrong. But then again, she said that she ran the place with her sisters, perhaps they're the ones who are running the bakery while she gets ready.

With nothing else for it, I make my way inside, instantly greeted by the sweet smell of baking pastry and an array of all kinds of sweet treats, far more than there are on her stall at the Christmas Fayre.

"Good evening," one of the women behind the counter says brightly. "What can I get for you?"

"Erm, I'm actually here to pick up Rowen," I admit.

Her eyes light up. "Ah, so you're Edward," she responds. "I'm Clover, pleased to meet you." She holds out her hand for me to shake.

"Nice to meet you. I'm guessing you're one of the sisters."

"The best one," she responds with a wide smile.

"Hardly," the blue-haired woman next to her says before turning back to her customer.

I chuckle at the clearly affectionate teasing.

"I'll just go see where she is," Clover says. "Or if she wants me to get rid of you."

I nod, certainly hoping that the latter isn't true. With nothing else to do, I take a look at the cakes on display. They're all beautifully crafted, and I can see minute differences in style that makes me wonder if each of the siblings have their own speciality when it comes to cake.

The door behind the counter opens and Rowen steps out. Her gaze falls on me and her whole face lights up in a smile. "Hey."

"Hi."

Her sisters seem somewhat surprised by the whole interaction, but I ignore them. Rowen slips on her coat and comes around the counter, brushing back a strand of her loose auburn hair. It's almost strange to see her with it down, but it looks good.

"Shall we?" she says, gesturing for the door.

I nod and open it for her, allowing her to step through.

"I'm sorry about them," she says once we're walking away from the bakery. "I'd have asked you to pick me up somewhere else, but considering I live there, I don't really have any other options."

"Do you all live at the bakery?"

"Oh, definitely not." She chuckles at the mere thought. "I live there, Ash lives at the academy during term time and with our parents during the holidays. My sisters all have their own places, thankfully. Can you imagine working together *and* living together? I had enough of that in my teens."

"I hope your parents had enough space for you all."

She nods. "Their house is amazing. Far too big for just me, but while we were growing up, it was perfect."

"How come they haven't downsized?" I ask, thinking of my own parents' choice to move into a smaller home.

"I think they're hoping for grandkids to fill it."

I raise an eyebrow. Brave of her to bring up kids on a first date. "Will they get them?"

"Probably. I wouldn't be surprised if Oakley has enough for the rest of us to get off the hook completely." She smiles. "She met her boyfriend six months ago, but if you saw them together, you'd never realise it, they act like they've been together for years. I wouldn't be surprised if we have a wedding by this time next year."

"That is fast."

"She's the *when you know, you know* kind of person."

"David was like that when he met Freddie," I respond. "We were living together when they went on their first date and I still remember him coming back from it and announcing this was the man he was going to marry."

"Did he?"

I nod. "Three years ago, they were blissfully happy. It'd be sickening if I wasn't so happy for them."

"I know how you feel," she responds. "So, where are we going?"

"That depends."

"On?"

"Well I thought ice skating would be a good date, it's fun, but not too intimate so won't make you feel rushed. But then I realised that you might hate ice skating, or not think it was a good idea, so then I was going to suggest doing something else, though I'll admit I have no idea what."

"You really want to go ice skating, huh?" Amusement comes through her voice, which makes me think that I haven't made a terrible miscalculation.

"Only if you don't mind."

"It sounds nice," she admits. "And like something I wouldn't normally do. Then again, this entire date is that."

"Because you don't normally say yes to people you just met, or because you don't date?"

"Both. But so far, I'm glad I'm stepping out of my comfort zone."

"I'll take that as a compliment."

"It was meant as one," she agrees. "So, ice skating. Don't we have to go out of town for that?"

I shake my head. "There's a temporary rink up opposite the Christmas Fayre, I'm surprised you haven't noticed it."

"Honestly, I'm mostly worrying about things like if I've got enough produce with me when I'm arriving, and if I've worked hard enough when I'm leaving."

"Do you ever take a break?"

"Sometimes. But mostly when one of my sisters makes me."

"I used to be like that. Then David talked some sense into me. That's when I started helping out at the vineyard."

"So your way of taking a break from work is by doing more work, just of a different kind?" Her lips quirk up into a smile.

"When you put it like that, it sounds bad."

"A little, but that's my kind of solution," she says. "Erm, I hate to break it to you, but the ice skating might have to go on hold." She holds out her hand just as a large drop of rain lands on it.

"Just my luck," I mutter. "I didn't bring an umbrella either."

"Luckily we don't need one," she reminds me, pulling her wand out of her pocket and summoning a magical shield above us just as the rain starts pounding down harder. "How do you feel about eggnog and mince pies?" she asks.

"They're good," I respond warily.

"Then come on, I know just the place where we can wait out the rain." She reaches out and grabs hold of my hand in hers and pulls me around the corner.

I go along willingly. She clearly knows the town centre better than I do, and when it comes to matters of food, I'm more than inclined to trust her.

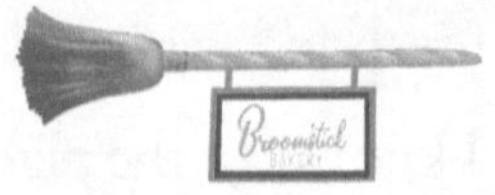

CHAPTER 8

ROWEN

The warm feeling in my stomach is better than any I've ever had conjured by magical cakes, even those that Oakley makes infused with the feel of a first kiss.

I wonder how similar that feeling is going to be.

A fierce blush rises to my cheeks at the thought. At least I don't have to worry about Edward noticing, my cheeks are probably already red from the bitter night wind as we walk slowly back through town towards the bakery. I wish I could think of something else for us to do so that the date doesn't have to end here, but I don't seem able to think of anything other than walking as slowly as I possibly can.

"I have to admit, those were some of the best mince pies I've ever tasted," Edward admits. "Though I've never tasted yours."

"We don't actually make them," I admit. "Though Hazel does a twist on a mince pie pain-aux-raisin that's to die for. I can bring one for you tomorrow, if you want?" I'm not sure what makes me offer, perhaps it's just enjoying the excuse to see and speak to him again that's spurring me on.

I need to get a grip on myself. I'm not this person usually, and I'm not sure how to deal with the sudden shift within me. Somehow, I'm inclined to blame this all on Oakley, though knowing her, she'll probably take that as a compliment and not an insult. I know what she's like.

"You don't make mince pies?" The surprise in his voice rivals that of Granny's the first Christmas we told her we weren't planning on doing them. She'll never admit it to us, but I think there's a part of her that's never forgiven us for taking them off the menu. "Wouldn't you sell hundreds of them?"

"Probably. But they're not any better than the ones we just had, so we made the decision to leave them off our festive menu to make room for other things. People can go anywhere for mince pies, but they can only get some of our stuff from us."

"That's rather extreme, don't you think?"

"Not really. We have a unique set of skills, that's what makes the bakery different from everywhere else. We have the advantage of each being able to specialise in one kind of baking, instead of being restricted to what one person is capable of. I'd never be able to reach Hazel's level of sophistication in patisserie, and I wouldn't know where to start with Clover's baklava, but they also wouldn't make biscuits that are any-where near as good as mine."

"You always sound so proud when you talk about them."

"You sound the same when you talk about David," I respond. "It is David, right?"

He chuckles. "Yes. It's David. And I suppose I do. Not what you expected from a barrister, right?"

"I try not to expect specific things from specific people," I respond.

"And yet you do."

"Fair point. I think everyone has expectations of some kind or other. Am I what you expect from a professional baker?" I ask.

"Absolutely, yes." There isn't a hint of malice in his voice. If anything, there's a mix of admiration and respect. "You're dedicated to your craft, hard-working, and judging from the time, you're a morning person."

"I am. Or at least, I think I am. I sometimes wonder if that's not true and I've just trained myself to act like I'm a morning person."

"I don't think that's possible. You can force yourself to get up, but I don't think it's possible to completely bypass what your natural rhythm is."

"Good point. I hope you're not a night person, or this is never going to work."

He chuckles. "I like to go for five am runs before I have to get ready for the day."

"Then you're my kind of person." While the admission itself doesn't surprise me, especially after how easy it's been to talk to him the entire time, the fact

I say it out loud *is* a surprise. I'm not normally so forward, but something about Edward is making me bold.

I wish I knew what it was.

"Oh, we're here," I say, realising we've reached the bakery already. A part of me is disappointed that the date is coming to an end already. A part of me wants to invite him inside for a drink or something, but I'm worried that will give the wrong impression, especially as it's only our first date.

"So we are."

The two of us stand still, staring at one another and waiting for the other person to make a move. I try to ignore the growing frustration inside me that I can't just act and need to think things through far more than any of my siblings do. I dismiss the thought. That's unfair. They're all perfectly cautious in their own way, and that doesn't make it any less valid than my way.

Edward steps forward, the expression on his face more intense than I've seen it before. Despite thinking about this moment multiple times over the course of our date, panic flits through me and I duck out of the way.

"So, goodnight," I say quickly, pulling out my wand and waving it at the door to unlock it. "I'll see you tomorrow."

Confusion rushes over his face, but he hides it before I can say anything about it. "I'll see you tomorrow." His disappointment comes through his voice, and it's echoed within me at the same time.

I force a smile onto my face and slip through the door before I do anything stupid. I flick my wand in the direction of the lock, not moving until I hear the tell tale click of it slipping into place.

I close my eyes and lean against the wall, letting out a frustrated groan.

"What's wrong with me?" I mutter, half expecting there to actually be someone around to answer. But that isn't the case.

My family may be nosey about how my date has gone, but at least they have the decency to wait until the morning to grill me about it. Though how I'm going to explain to them what just happened is beyond me, especially when I'm not sure I have an explanation myself.

And I might have just ruined something that could have been meaningful to me.

I breathe out deeply. What's done is done. I'll take one of the pain-aux-raisins for him, just like I said I would, and hope that it's enough to convince him that I made a mistake and to give me another chance.

CHAPTER 9

ROWEN

Even though the fayre has just opened, it's still busy enough to almost take my mind off the disastrous end to my date with Edward last night. I just don't understand what I was thinking when I ducked out of the way.

"Hey, Rowen."

I look up, half hoping to see Edward standing on the other side of the stall despite it being a woman's voice saying my name. Instead, I'm greeted by my dark-haired cousin.

"Hey." I wave to her and Azíl.

"You have things here that you do not have at the shop," Azíl says, his eyes wide as he takes in the array of cakes and sweet treats on display.

I chuckle. "We do. But they'll be at the shop once the fayre is over," I promise. "And you can have as many as you like now."

His whole face lights up.

Willow shakes her head in bemusement, and I assume this isn't the first time she's dealing with this reaction from him this holiday season. Especially considering how much he loves food, and that it'll be his first-ever Christmas. From what Clover has said, Willow is determined to make it special for him.

"Rowen?" Willow asks.

"Hmm?"

"I asked how the fayre was going, but you didn't answer."

"Oh, sorry, I didn't hear you."

"Yeah, that was clear. And not like you. What's going on?" The concern on her face is impossible to miss.

I glance over to where Azíl and Ash are chatting happily about the various cakes we have on the stall. "Do you think Ash wants to join the bakery?" I blurt out.

Willow frowns, clearly not having expected the question. "Have you asked him?"

"No. Oakley said she thought he might."

"He hasn't said anything to me, but I remember how you were when we were his age, you'd do everything you could to help your Grandma at the shop. Everything. Because it's what you wanted more than anything."

"I remember. What's your point?"

"When is the last time Ash said no to anything related to the shop?"

"I can't think of one."

"Exactly. Maybe talk to him about it and see what he says. But if he's anything like you, and I've always suspected that he is, then this is going to be exactly what he wants."

"Hmm, when did you get so wise?"

"I have a great teacher." She flashes a happy smile in Azíl's direction. "He's changed my entire life."

"Do you ever regret it?"

She shakes her head. "It's been hard, and I doubt it's over, but when I think back on the past nine months, all I can think of is that we succeeded and he's free of his curse. Now he can live his life like any other normal thirty-two-year-old."

"I don't think Azíl would ever be considered normal."

"Hmm, true, but he'll get there. Now, you're distracting me from the real situation at hand. What's bothering you? Because I doubt it's Ash and his desire to join the bakery."

I sigh. She's closest with Clover by far, but we were in the same year at school, and later when we went onto Grimalkin Academy together, so we've spent enough time together for me to consider Willow someone I'll trust with my secrets.

The only thing I'm unsure of is whether I'm ready to actually share this one.

"You don't have to tell me," she says quickly. "I can pretend I saw nothing and carry on."

I let out a loud sigh. "It's not that, I just don't really know how to explain."

"Believe it or not, I'm getting really good at dealing with those kinds of things. Spill."

"I went on a date last night."

"Wow, I was not expecting that." She gives a soft chuckle. "Was your victim willing?"

"Of course he was. He asked me."

"Right, so what's the problem?"

I groan, trying to work out how I've gotten myself into this situation and what the best way out of it is. "The date was great, we seemed to be getting on well, which wasn't a surprise because we've been talking all week..."

"This is the only place you've been all week," she points out. "Ooh, have you started an affair with a rival bakery owner? That would be a lot of fun to watch."

"No. He's the brother of the mulled wine stall owner."

"Half disappointing. Carry on."

"When we were saying goodnight, I thought he was going to kiss me."

"Which is a good thing if the date went well," she says carefully. "Unless it didn't go well."

"It did."

"Oh, no, is he a bad kisser? Eesh, and now you have to see him."

"No. Well, I wouldn't know. I kind of ran away."

"You ran away?" she repeats.

"Yes." I close my eyes and let out a small groan of frustration. "I don't understand, I wanted to kiss him right up until that moment, and then I just freaked out and ran away. He sounded so disappointed."

"You do too," she points out.

"I am. I don't know what I was thinking."

"Me neither, it's unusual for you to date in the first place, which must mean you really like him." She cocks her head to the side and considers for a moment. "Have you talked to him yet?"

My gaze slips to the bagged-up mince pie pain-aux-raisins. "No."

"Then you should."

"But when? It's barely half-ten and we're already busy."

"Mmm, I must admit to being surprised. We came early so we're back at the coffee shop in time for the rush and it's still busier than I expected it to be. But it's fine. We have plenty of time to get back. Ash is here and in charge, and Azíl and I will lend him a hand until you're back."

I have to admit, her offer sounds tempting, even though I wouldn't normally relinquish control like that. "Are you sure?"

Surprise flits over her face. She must not have expected me to say yes either. "I'm sure. We know enough to sell, and we normally sell your cakes at the coffee shop anyway, so it's not like it's weird that we're suddenly doing it," she points out.

"Okay."

"That must have been some almost kiss."

"Everyone keeps telling me I need to relax more and do more things for me," I say.

"Yes, and we never expect you to actually do it. Hence the surprise. Now go on before you chicken out. We'll listen to everything Ash says and you'll have nothing to worry about," she promises.

I nod and grab the paper bag. "Thanks, Willow."

"Any time. Good luck."

I'm sure she's waving me off, but I'm no longer paying attention to the stall, or any of the people standing with it.

CHAPTER 10

ROWEN

The mulled wine stand is thankfully quiet enough that I don't have to awkwardly wait in line, and that, added to the knowledge that Willow will ask me what happened the moment I get back to our stall, means that I don't back out and run away again.

Which is probably a good thing. I can't imagine what Edward will think if I keep doing that, and it'll cut into my chances of persuading him to give me another chance significantly, something I really don't want to do.

He looks up from what he's doing and his gaze latches onto me, surprise flitting over his face in response.

"I'll be back in a moment," he says to the other man behind the stall. I assume that's his brother, but I seem to have made a big enough mistake that he's not introducing me. Which is deserved.

The other man nods and says something too quiet for me to hear while shooting a look in my direction. It seems that he knows what happened then. I don't know if that's a good thing or not.

Edward makes his way out from the stall and gestures for the two of us to take a seat on a nearby bench.

Nerves flutter in my stomach unbidden, reminding me of the chances of this going horribly wrong.

"Hey," I say.

"Hi."

"I brought you one of Hazel's pain-aux-raisins." I hold out the bag for him.

He manages a weak smile and takes it from me. "Thanks."

"I'm sorry," I blurt out. "About last night. I'm sorry that I bailed and ran away. And I'm even more sorry that I didn't think to turn around and actually talk to you about what was going on in my head."

He raises an eyebrow. "Okay..."

I take a deep breath. This is going to need more of an explanation and I'm not sure precisely where to start. "So, I don't date very much. And by very much I mean, at all. My sisters love to tease me about it."

"In the way only siblings can," he interjects.

"Precisely. I did have a relationship, but it ended about four years ago when he moved to America."

"I'm sorry, that must have been hard," Edward responds.

"Not really. Which is the problem. I think we were mostly with each other out of convenience. We didn't think that's what it was at the time, I even believed it was love for a while, but I don't think that's what it was. Or at least not romantic love. It was too easy for Mickey to leave for him to have loved me, and it was too easy for me to let him go for it to be love for me."

"Right."

"I haven't really dated since then," I admit. "Mickey was a great guy, and I suppose a part of me wonders if there's something wrong with me because I didn't love him. He treated me well, we had fun, everything was fine. It just wasn't the love everyone talks about. When you moved closer to me last night, all I could think about was what would happen if the same thing occurred."

"I see."

"And I'm sorry. I should have explained. Or at least done something."

He takes a deep breath. "I don't want you to do anything that makes you uncomfortable, Rowen."

"I know. That's the problem. Kind of. I mean, it's not a problem, I like that. But it's part of what's causing me to worry about the way things might progress. If you respect me and treat me well, and I'm going to settle and think that I feel something I don't?"

"Hmm. I can see why that would be enough to cause a freak-out. I guess the question is do you feel the same way about me as you did about Mickey when you first started dating?"

I think back, trying to recall the details of what it was like when I first met my ex, but mostly coming up with nothing. "I don't think so, but I can't remember it clearly enough to be sure."

"Okay, that's fair. A lot of time has passed."

"It has." I fiddle with the edge of my apron, partly wishing that I'd thought to take it off before coming here, especially as there's a risk this conversation could end up with me crying. That won't be a good look for the bakery. "But I think I feel differently," I whisper.

"What makes you think that?" His question seems to come from an honest and non-judgemental place, and I can tell that he's curious more than accusatory. Like he wants to know so he can help me work out what's going on in my head.

I appreciate that more than he can ever know.

"All I've thought about since I got inside the bakery last night is what an idiot I am and how I wanted to talk to you." It feels strange to admit something like that out loud to him, but also right at the same time.

Which *is* different to how things were with Mickey. We didn't have any huge problems, but it's safe to say that we never really talked about how we were feeling and that was a problem.

"Then I'd say that's a good sign," Edward says.

"And I wanted to ask you out on a do-over. Or a second date, depending on exactly what we want to call it. I was thinking ice skating?" I meet his gaze for the first time since I started talking.

He smiles at me and opens his mouth to respond but is cut off by a loud screech.

"You!" a woman yells.

We both turn to find a furious-looking middle-aged woman storming towards us.

"Me?" I ask.

"Yes, you. You work at Broomstick Bakery, right?" There's a seething note to her voice, which has me all kinds of confused.

"I do." I rise to my feet in an attempt to feel less exposed to the woman. "Would you like to come back to the stall and we can discuss the issue?"

"We can discuss the issue right here," she says, crossing her arms.

"Okay, how can I help?"

"Those samples you gave out taste disgusting. They're full of disappointment."

I frown. "Disappointment? That's not an emotion we'd ever use in any of our pastries."

"Well that's how it tastes. It makes me feel as if I've had the worst day imaginable. Why would I want to feel like that?"

"You wouldn't," I respond. "And I'm very sorry about that. If you'll come back to the stall with me, then I can get you something else as a replacement." Though if she's only talking about the samples we have on display, then I'm not really sure that's warranted. Maybe she's just trying to get a freebie out of us. It's happened before, and it'll happen again, especially because it works. The bad publicity that could come from someone spouting off about how our products don't do what they're supposed to will do a lot worse damage to our business than one or two free pastries.

"I don't want anything else from you." She turns on her heels and storms away before I can think of another way to appease her, leaving me staring after her both confused and upset by the situation.

"What was that about?" Edward asks.

"I have no idea," I whisper. "We have samples out, but they all taste fine. Oakley almost messed up a batch of cupcakes a few months back and we learned our lesson to sample everything afterwards." Tears sting the corners of my eyes.

To my surprise, Edward reaches out and pulls me into a hug. I lean into him, enjoying the warm scent that reaches my nose. There's a hint of the mulled wine spices he's been working with, but there's more to it than that, and I have to assume that the smell is uniquely his.

"All right, well the woman clearly doesn't want anything from you, so let's go back to the stall and check all the samples again. I'll do it too just to make sure, and we'll go from there," he says softly.

I nod. "Thank you. You don't have to come though."

"I want to, Rowen," he says. "And we weren't done with our conversation either. So how about I help you with this, and then we'll return to it?"

"Okay." I can't tell if I'm feeling more gratitude that he wants to help me fix the situation with the unhappy customer or relief that he's willing to talk more about the situation.

Either way, it gives me hope that I haven't ruined things before they've even got started.

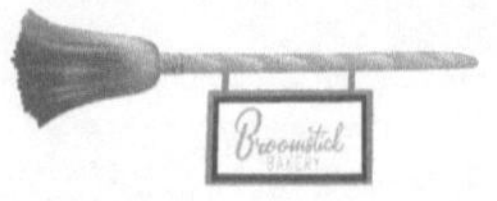

CHAPTER 11

ROWEN

The stall is reasonably busy by the time we get back to it, and I'm glad Willow and Azíl offered to stay to help Ash, especially as Azíl seems to be busy charming two little old ladies into buying far more Christmas cake than they can possibly need. I may need to ask him what his secret is, though I suspect the answer is a charming accent and an enthusiasm for cake that can only come with having discovered it within the past year.

"Hey, Edward, good to see you back," Ash says brightly.

Willow whips her head around and raises an eyebrow, but doesn't say anything. I'm sure I'll hear whatever is on her mind later.

"Do you have the samples that we've been giving out?" I ask Ash.

"Huh, yeah sure." He searches for the plate and passes it over to us. "What's going on?"

"A woman just came and accused me of the samples I gave her being bad."

Ash frowns. "We haven't given out any samples today."

"Not even since I left?"

"Azíl does the selling of twenty samples," he points out.

I snort, while the man in question beams with pride.

Willow shakes her head in bemusement. "Unfortunately, speaking of selling, we're going to need to get going if we want to get back to the coffee shop in time to open up."

I frown. "That's late for you, isn't it?"

"I wanted to make the most of the time before Azíl goes back to Morocco, so I put a sign on the door saying we were at the Christmas Fayre for the morning. I doubt it'll have caused too much of an issue." She shrugs and looks at her boyfriend. "You ready?"

He nods.

"Don't forget your wages," Ash says, holding up a box of cakes.

Azíl's eyes light up and he takes it from my brother. They say their goodbyes and head towards the exit.

"Isn't that the owner of Cauldron Coffee Shop?" Edward asks.

"She's our cousin," I respond.

"Talented family."

"Mmhmm. Right, samples." I hold out the plate to him.

"Do you really think there's something wrong with them?" Ash asks.

"I don't know, but it's always better to check."

"That's true, but we still haven't given out any samples today, I don't see how anyone could have taken offence at them," he responds.

"Maybe they tried one yesterday?" I think back, trying to recall if I remember giving any to the woman in question, but it seems unlikely. For a start, there's nothing wrong with how any of the samples taste, and secondly, if the emotion in the sample had gone wrong, then it would already have worn off by now.

"Look, why don't you two keep testing things here, and I'll see what I can find out in the rest of the fayre," Edward says.

"Are you sure? I don't want to take you away from your brother's stall?"

"David will be fine, we won't hit our busiest part of the day for hours yet, and I'll stop by and talk to him before I carry on investigating."

I reach out and touch his arm. "Thank you."

"I'm glad I can help," he murmurs, the words seeming to be just meant for me.

"I really appreciate it." A small part of me wants to ask whether this means he's going to agree to the make-up date with me, but I know the time isn't right for that.

"I'll be back as soon as I can."

It's only once he's gone that I realise how close we were standing.

"I have so many questions," Ash says, amusement coming through his tone.

"And you'll get no answers."

"Oh, so when you're all interfering with my love life, it's fine, but when I want to know about yours, it's not?"

I wrinkle my nose. "Don't say things like that, it makes it sound weird."

"These taste fine," Ash says, gesturing to the samples.

"I know they are."

"Do you think the woman could have made a mistake?" he asks.

I let out a loud sigh. "She asked about the bakery by name, I don't see how she could have been mistaken about it."

"Hmm."

"What are you thinking?"

"Nothing helpful."

"Then you can tell me anyway."

"What if it's someone trying to rile you up? We're spending time dealing with this when we could be spending time selling." Ash restocks a row of gingerbread men.

I sigh. "That's a possibility, but I don't see how we can ignore it either way."

"And that's the genius of it. At least we have Edward to help, they didn't plan for that," Ash says jovially.

"You're very upbeat this morning. What happened with Ellie?"

"Oh, so you can ask about my girlfriend but I can't ask about what's going on with you and the mulled wine guy?"

"Yes. You're my little brother, that's exactly how it works," I point out.

"Nothing happened with Ellie," he responds. "I've just been enjoying working the Christmas Fayre. The atmosphere is really good this year."

"It is," I agree, eyeing him with interest. Now that Oakley and Willow have pointed it out, I have to admit that I'm starting to see clues about Ash's feelings towards the bakery all over the place.

Now I just need to find a good way to bring it up without it seeming forced.

Or worse, like the others have told me I need to.

CHAPTER 12

EDWARD

The fayre is getting busier by the minute, which is making it more and more difficult to find anything. I try to ignore the frustration growing within me that I can't find a way to help Rowen. The look on her face when she thought she'd disappointed a customer was heartbreaking. Almost as much as hearing about how she's scared that she doesn't know how to love. I'm not even sure how to deal with that one, but I suppose that's part of what scared her.

And I don't want to prove her right about her feelings by pushing her away because of one avoided kiss. I should have asked if it was okay before I tried to initiate something, and I'll remember that next time.

I push thoughts of her aside and focus on trying to discover what the actual cause of her disgruntled customer might be. Something tells me that it's not about the samples she's been handing out, especially if her brother is certain that they haven't handed any out.

Which leaves two options. Deliberate sabotage, or a misunderstanding. I'm not sure which is the most preferable. Sabotage has to be dealt with, but a misunderstanding could have further reaching consequences.

I try not to let the frustration of not finding an immediate answer get to me. Normally, I'm good at being patient, I have to be in my line of work, but right now, I'm feeling increasingly agitated by the idea of this dragging on longer than it has to.

Perhaps it's simply because my conversation with Rowen was interrupted for this. And while I'm not regretting helping her with the problem, I do wish that we could have had a chance to finish talking first.

A flash of the same blue aprons Rowen and Ash wear catches my eye and I make my way through the crowd towards the person wearing it, half dreading what I'm going to find. I don't want to be the one that goes and tells Rowen that someone is trying to sabotage her bakery. I can tell how much it means to her, and I don't want her to have to go through that. Though at least I have the legal knowledge to help her through the situation if it comes to it, and that comes with the distinct advantage of being able to spend more time with her.

"Excuse me," I call out.

The young man in the blue apron turns to me and smiles. "Hi, would you like to try a sample?" he asks, holding out a platter.

"What are they?" I ask.

"Bah-Humbug sweets. We're selling them over at stand sixty-seven."

I frown. "Sixty-seven?"

He nods.

I pull out the map of the fayre. "Isn't sixty-seven Broomstick Bakery?"

"No, no, it's Doctor Joke."

"Doctor Joke?" I repeat.

"Yes. We make magical practical jokes for stocking fillers."

"And you're at stand sixty-seven?"

"Yes."

"I don't think you are," I say, looking down at the map. "Look, sixty-seven is Broomstick Bakery. It's my friend's stall." I show him.

His face turns white.

"She's been dealing with angry customers because of how your sweets made them feel."

The man's eyes widen. "But we're at sixty-seven."

"No, you're at seventy-six," I respond, pointing it out on the map.

"Eurgh numbers have never been my strong suit. I'll make sure I'm telling people the right number from now on," he promises.

"Can you come explain to my friend too?" I ask. "I don't think she's going to relax until she hears it was just an accident." Though there's still going to be a lot to clear up once that's done.

"Erm, I'm not really supposed to leave my post. My boss won't be happy."

"I don't think he's going to be happy knowing that you've been sending people to the wrong store either, but you'd better tell them so they don't think that your samples aren't doing their job. Based on what people are saying to my friend, they're doing exactly what you say they will." There's a part of me that wants to try the sweets even if they'll put me in a bad mood. Not that I need the help considering this man's bad knowledge of numbers has made problems for Rowen that weren't necessary. She's made it clear just how important the fayre is for the bakery's business all year around. This could have terrible consequences.

"Oh, erm, I'm not sure," the man murmurs.

"Look, if you take responsibility for it, everyone can start mopping up the damage," I point out. "If you try to hide the mistake, it's only going to get worse for you." I'm trying to be careful about not tipping over the edge into threatening him, especially when that's not what I want to do. I just want for him to take responsibility so we can fix the issue. "I'm sure there'll be free cake in it for you."

He perks up at that. "Free cake? All right, you've persuaded me." He puts the sweets into a tin. "Lead the way."

I breathe a sigh of relief, unsure exactly which one of my suggestions worked, but glad of it all the same.

I set off back through the fayre, nodding to the people I recognise after a few days here. It's amazing how tight-knit the community of vendors seems to be. If I come back next year, maybe I'll be lucky enough to get to know more of them better. The large Christmas tree that dominates the square comes into view, and I check that my follower is still coming. Somehow, I wouldn't be surprised if he finds a way to disappear off into the crowd and not explain himself. I suppose that won't be the end of the world. It's not like Rowen won't believe me when I tell her what happened, I'm the one who always feels the need to have evidence and witnesses.

Besides, I think she'll be interested in the Bah-Hum-bug sweets and what they're capable of.

Relief fills me as the crowd in front of us parts and I get a glimpse of the Broomstick Bakery stand. I can tell Rowen is stressed even from this distance and this short of a time knowing her, but she's also busy dealing with a small surge of customers, making me certain that the young man beside me hasn't caused irreparable damage and the whole situation can still be salvaged with a little bit of planning.

At least, that's what I'm hoping.

CHAPTER 13

ROWEN

I force a tight smile onto my face while I listen to the explanation of how the woman ended up blaming us for the way Doctor Joke's Bah-Humbug sweets made her feel.

"I didn't mean to cause any problems," the man in front of me says. "I'm just not good at numbers."

"Maybe next time you should stick with saying the name of your stall." My words come out harsher than I intend them to, but given the circumstances, he's lucky that I'm not screaming. That's what I feel like doing.

"Oh, I hadn't thought of that."

I bunch my hand into a fist and just nod. "Please excuse me." I need to step away before I say or do anything I regret.

"I'll deal with this," Ash promises me.

It's almost enough to make me turn around and face the cause of my issues just so that my little brother doesn't have to do it, but I need to remember that he's an adult, and if he's going to join the bakery properly, then I need to trust him to handle things like this.

"Thanks, Ash."

Surprise flits over his face, followed by determination. It's definitely a good thing if he's the one who takes charge of the situation. He's probably feeling calmer simply because he's not the one who got yelled at.

And he's not the one responsible for everyone.

I head out of the back of the stall and lean against the wooden edge, letting out a shaky breath. It's rare times like this when I wonder whether it would have been soothing to take up smoking, but I know it's bad for me.

"Mind if I join you?" Edward asks.

I smile tightly. "Be my guest, though I can't say I'm the best company."

"I think you're just fine."

"Then you have bad taste in women."

"Quite the contrary. You're angry because you care about your work."

"I don't think I'm angry as much as frustrated and annoyed. It's such a stupid mistake, but it could have cost us a customer. Probably more than one."

"You'll catch them some other way," he assures me.

"You don't know that."

"Okay, true. But every time I come to your stall, you're dealing with new people. That suggests you're not hurting for customers."

I sigh. "I know that's logical, but sometimes it doesn't feel like that's the case. I used to set goals for the bakery and I'd tell myself that I'd be happy when we hit them and not need more. But that's never actually happened. Every time I reach one of those goals, I'm happy for a second, and then it becomes not enough and I reach for the next thing."

"I think that's called being ambitious."

"It feels like a bad thing."

"Sure, if you want to stay a small family-run business and you have fun just baking. But there's nothing wrong with wanting more than that. There's nothing wrong with wanting a global brand."

"That might be a bit far," I say.

"Okay, well there's nothing wrong with wanting a national brand. And with all of you involved in the bakery, I don't see why you can't achieve that."

"You haven't even met one of my sisters."

"And I barely know the others," he agrees. "But I'd like to think I've gotten a good glimpse of you, and I've seen Ash in action. He's nineteen and he's here every day selling cakes and acting like he wants to be here. That's impressive. I'm pretty sure when I was nineteen all I wanted to do was party and sleep in."

"Was that common in law school?"

"Incredibly. But you know what? Despite having a career of my own, I still feel the bite of ambition when it comes to the vineyard. I want it to do even better than it's already doing, even though that's already pretty good."

"That kind of makes me feel better," I admit.

"I thought it might."

"Maybe next year we could do some kind of collaboration around Christmas?" I suggest. "We can do a hamper. Maybe we can even get some of the other regular Christmas Fayre vendors involved."

"I can see that being really popular," he agrees. "Though probably not if it includes Bah-Humbug sweets."

I let out a strangled laugh. "Definitely not. Why would people even want that?"

"I'm not sure," he admits. "I assume to play a trick on someone."

I wrinkle my nose, unimpressed by the implications of using magical confections to trick people. This is why the whole industry should be better legislated, though I doubt I'm the person to spearhead that.

"What am I going to do about the damage they've caused now?" I ask. "I know we still have customers, but right now, there are other fayre goers who have tasted these sweets and think that we're responsible for it. I know that the best thing to do is to actively change the perspective of those people, but I have no idea how."

Edward's eyes light up. "What if we tried a collaboration right now?"

"I like the idea, but I don't know how that's going to help us."

"Simple. We'll fight samples with samples. I know it's just you and Ash here right now, but can you get a couple of other people here?"

"Probably." Between my sisters and Willow, I'm sure two or three of them might be able to come lend a hand.

"Then let's get them here and then we can prepare mulled wine and biscuit samples. That way it gives me an excuse to help too."

"I have stolen you away from David a lot today."

"He won't mind. He might tease me for it, but what are siblings for."

I let out a snort of amusement. "Mine would say exactly the same thing."

"So let me go talk to him and sort out samples, you deal with your end and we'll reconvene back here in about half an hour. Then we'll give out as many samples as we possibly can."

"Thank you," I say, realising that I feel much better now that I can do something about the situation.

"Hey, this benefits the vineyard too, remember?"

"Mmhmm. We'll have to make sure to switch our supplier to say thanks."

"I'm sure my Dad would be happy with that," he admits.

"Okay, so I'll see you in a bit?" I linger, unsure precisely what the best way to say goodbye is. There's something hanging in the air between us, a closeness that I don't think I've ever experienced with anyone before, but I'm not sure how to deal with it, or what it means for me or for us.

Edward lifts a hand but then thinks better of it and lets it fall to his side. "I'll see you in a bit," he echoes, waving and heading off in the direction of the mulled wine stand.

I let out a frustrated sigh. I feel like that would have been the perfect moment for *something*, even if I'm not completely sure what it would have been. But I wasted it.

I push the thought to the side. For one, I need to focus on damage control and make sure that our reputation doesn't get ruined by someone else's mistake.

And for another, if this goes well, then we're going to be seeing a lot more of it, especially if we can work on a collaboration between our two family businesses.

CHAPTER 14

ROWEN

The queue is bigger than I've seen it since arriving at the fayre, and I start to worry about whether we're going to have enough cakes to manage the situation.

The door at the back of the stall opens and Ellie steps inside, sparing a small smile for Ash as she passes. The two of them are cute together, and even more so because they're acting like this is the work environment it is.

"I'm going to need more samples," she says.

"The tray's over there, ready to go." I point it out to her. "You just need to..."

"Head over to David and get fresh mulled wine samples from him. I know. They're going down well," she assures me. "And it seems like you're busy here."

"Very. Now we're worried about the cake," Ash puts in.

"I saw Hazel unloading the van a few minutes ago," Ellie says. "So I imagine it won't be a problem for long."

I breathe a sigh of relief. If Hazel's here, that means they've decided to offload a lot of what's still out at the bakery on us, which is good considering how busy it is here. The bakery will be closing in about an hour anyway, whereas we still have another three to trade in.

"Is there a special event tonight?" Ash asks.

"I don't think so," Ellie responds. "But it's the last Friday before the fayre ends, I imagine everyone who wanted to come but hasn't yet has turned up."

Ash nods and turns to the next customer with one last smile for his girlfriend.

"Thanks for helping out, Ellie," I say.

"It's no problem. I enjoy it." She smiles reassuring-ly at me, and I find I actually believe her, though I suspect part of what makes her happy to help is her relationship to my brother.

She disappears out of the stall just as Hazel arrives with two trays of cakes. "Where do you want these and where do you want me?" my youngest sister asks.

"You're not heading back to the bakery?"

She shakes her head as she sets the trays down in the spot I indicate to. "Clover's on her way down too, she's just closing up. It's dead in the town centre, and by the looks of it, this is why. Might as well have all the manpower you can, right?"

I breathe a sigh of relief. "You don't know how glad I am to hear that. Do you want to be handing out samples or selling?"

"Oh, tough choice. You and Ash know what you're doing here, and you're a good team. I'll head out for samples."

"Okay, we need another tray setting up, then you need to go to the mulled wine stall just down from here. David will sort you out with samples from him."

"Do you know this David well?"

"Only in passing. It's his brother that I know."

"Wait, is the brother the one you went on a date with?" she asks.

I bite my bottom lip and give her a reluctant nod.

"And you're working with the stall now? That's a good sign."

"Now isn't the time, Hazel," I remind her.

"Right, but you're going to tell us all everything tomorrow, especially as you've roped us all in to help now."

"You get a share of the profits," I remind her.

She chuckles. "So I do. Oh, Antonio might be down in a bit too. He's having an early dinner with his dad, but he said he'd come give us a hand if we still need it once he's done."

"He's going to regret getting involved with a Parkes by the time we're done with him."

Hazel snorts. "Hardly. He knows a thing or two about the culinary world and how it works, this is all part of it for him," she reminds me as she breaks up a couple of the biscuits from the tray she brought and lays them out on a sample tray while I fill the display cases with them. "Besides, it seems like the Parkes clan is about to have another victim." She nods towards the crowd.

I look up and meet Edward's gaze from where he's standing opposite. He lifts his free hand and gives a wave.

A smile springs to my face and I return the gesture, letting out a small sigh.

"Wow, you have it bad." Amusement dances in Hazel's voice.

"It's just a crush," I mutter.

"So? That's how these things start. You find something you like about someone, then you get to know them better and realise that more than just the surface stuff lines up, and then you decide to make it into a relationship."

"You decide? It doesn't just happen?"

"Why would it just happen? These things take work."

"Hmm. Oakley said the same."

"You seem surprised? Oakley loves love, but she's realistic enough to know that it takes more than that to make something last," Hazel says. "Right, that's me sorted. Are you all set for ill-timed sisterly advice?"

"I'm not sure about that, I might need some more."

"Then it's going to have to wait or I think Ash's head might explode." She nods in his direction, and sure enough, my brother seems to be struggling with the demand from the customers.

Hazel heads out of the back of the stall to collect her mulled wine sample and I jump into serving. I'm glad she thought to bring more products from the bakery.

"Hi, do you have any of the Christmas Pudding macarons left?" a man in a tweed jacket asks.

"Let me just check." I do a quick scan of the display case, half surprised to discover that we don't. "I'm sorry, we seem to have sold out, but we have several other flavours."

"What would you suggest?"

"If you don't have a favourite flavour, I can give you a selection of six of what we've got." Which is far safer than promising something specific only for me to realise we don't have it. I haven't even begun to unpack some of Hazel's boxes yet.

"Sure, that sounds good. They're for my girlfriend, she loves macarons."

"Then I can put it in a gift box for you too if you'd like."

His eyes light up. "Yes, please."

I smile and head to the trays to search out six macarons, pleased to find there are multiple flavours of the bright confections hiding within them. Hazel and Clover must have just emptied the bakery fridges and brought everything here.

I finish sorting out the box and hand it over to the man, taking payment from him and moving onto the next customer. Despite the fact we're fast running out of the products we planned on selling at the fayre, we're not having to turn many people away, and it's quickly becoming obvious just how well Ash knows what we do. He's suggesting alternatives with just as much ease as I am, and is answering almost every question without any input from our sisters. I have to admit to being impressed. And a little annoyed at myself that I didn't notice how passionate he was before this.

"Hey."

I look up to find Edward stepping inside the stall and my heart skips a beat. "Hi. You doing okay out there?"

He nods. "Just needed a sample refill. And maybe an excuse for a breather."

"It's hectic out there."

"It is, I thought we were busy earlier in the week, but it's nothing compared to this."

"We'll be better prepared next year," I say, though I'm not sure whether that's going to be true or not. I suspect that the Christmas Fayre is going to be one of those events where we never quite know what to expect. "How is David doing?"

"Well. Freddie finished work an hour ago, so they're manning the stall together now and having a great time with it."

"Somehow, we made this whole thing into a real family affair," I joke.

He chuckles. "It did get more out of hand than I expected. Now I should get back out there. We only have an hour left before the fayre closes and I see you still have stuff left to sell."

"Not that much more. And we'll have a tough morning ahead of us tomorrow to try and make enough to restock both the stall and the shop." I fill his platter with a selection of samples, barely paying attention to what's what anymore. I know everything tastes good, and that everything will give the eater a positive emotional experience, and that's all it needs to do until they're here looking for something specific.

"But you love it, don't you?"

I can't help the wide smile that spreads over my face. "Like nothing else."

"Then I'm glad I get to share it with you." He picks up his tray, lingering for a moment as if he wants to say something else, but stopping before he does and heading out the door.

I sigh wistfully, looking forward to a chance for the two of us to sit down and actually be able to talk away from the customers.

One more hour, and then we'll get our chance.

# CHAPTER 15

ROWEN

By the time there's half an hour left to go before the fayre closes, we have almost nothing left, and the amount of customers we have has dwindled as a result. Which is probably a good thing, especially as we've already sent our sisters off to enjoy themselves, leaving just me, Ash, and Ellie at the stall. I'd have sent her away too, but I think part of why she agreed to help us out is so that she got to spend time with Ash. The two of them don't get a lot of time together between his work for me at the fayre, and her internship, they'll probably appreciate half an hour to take in the fayre themselves.

Ash hands over the last packet of gingerbread men to the customer he's dealing with, going through all of the motions that come with customer service. He's very good at it, which makes a lot of sense since he's young and charming. That can go a long way when it comes to dealing with people.

"Hey, Ellie," I say to get her attention.

"What's up? Do you want me to move some stuff or pack away?"

I shake my head. "I was wondering if you'd like to actually enjoy what's left of the fayre."

"Only if you're sure you can spare us. I hate to think of you having to deal with everything alone."

"It's fine. There's time left and I can do things slowly," I assure her. "But it's sweet of you to say that." Especially as it isn't her family business.

I glance at Ash. *Yet*. Perhaps it's early for them to be thinking of that kind of thing, but I've been certain that Ash and Ellie are the real deal since the first time he introduced us to her, even if he claimed they were just friends.

His customer leaves and I see my chance to let them leave. "I can probably manage by myself now. There's not much left and things are winding down."

"Actually, there's something Ash wanted to talk to you about," Ellie says, taking me by surprise.

Panic fills me for a brief moment as I consider all the things my little brother could need my help with. I don't think there's anything we can't deal with, but it's still scary to think of the possibilities. "Is everything all right? Do you need me to talk to Mum and Dad about something?"

"No, they can't help with this." He's nervous, I can sense it.

"Then what is it? Something at the academy?"

"Rowen," Ash says, a surprisingly firm note in his voice. "It's nothing bad. It's just that I've been doing some thinking and I want to join the bakery."

Surprise fills me despite the fact my sisters and Willow have all been preparing me for this moment. I suppose there's a part of me that wasn't ready to believe it before I heard him say the words. "You do?"

He nods. "I've wanted it for a while, but seeing Ellie work at her internship, it's made me certain that this is what I want to do."

"I see." Eurgh, I'm going about this all wrong. I should be acting more excited, especially when I think it's going to be a great thing, both for him, and for the bakery. "I'll have to talk to the others. But your ideas for the children's range went down well, I don't think they'll have any problem with it."

"For real?" His whole face lights up as he says it, making me believe everything all of them have been telling me.

"Yes, for real," I assure him. "You're our brother, Ash. If this is what you really want, then of course we want you at the bakery. *After* you finish studying."

"Thank you."

"Now, go enjoy the rest of the fayre. You'll have plenty of time to work overtime once you're part of the bakery properly." Though I'm not going to work him too hard, we're a team and we all make sure everyone gets enough time off.

"Are you sure you're all right if we leave you?" He glances around at the scattered boxes and assortment of dirty tongs that have been abandoned in a bucket to be sent back to the bakery for cleaning. It's certainly not as neat and tidy as I'd like it to be, but after the day we've had, I think that's to be expected.

"Yes. Go have fun." I wave them away before he says something that risks me changing my mind.

"Thanks, Row." He takes off his apron and drops it into the box under the counter. I close my eyes and try not to let how much work I'm going to have to do when we get back to the bakery overwhelm me. I should have prepared better for a situation like this.

But it's fine. It's all about learning, and next year, I won't make the same mistake.

I watch the two of them leave with a smile on my face. They're sweet together, and I like that Ellie is supporting him in going after what he wants. But secretly, I'm even more excited that Ash is going to be joining the bakery. We were all so careful to try not to force baking onto him when he was small, and yet none of us paid enough attention to know that it was something he wanted.

I let out a sigh and pull myself away from watching. With no customers to tend to, I start tidying the stall, pleased with how fast the progress is despite my aching muscles and overall exhaustion.

"Rowen?"

I turn around to find Edward standing on the other side of the stall with two steaming mugs of mulled wine in his hands.

I reach up and tuck a strand of stray hair behind my ear. "Hey."

"Ash said you were almost done for the night, and I figured you were probably quiet if you let him leave."

"Let is a strong word, I'd say I encouraged him to."

He chuckles, the sound as warm and inviting as the first time I heard it. "Can I come in?"

"Considering you've brought me a drink, it would be rude of me to say no, wouldn't it?" I tease.

"That was my plan."

I gesture for him to come join me, pulling the fold-up chairs around so we don't have to continue standing but not taking a seat. "Thank you for all your help today," I say. "If you hadn't found the Bah-Humbug guy and then helped talk me down, I don't think we'd have sold half as much as we did."

"Hey, you helped our business too. David said he made more today than he did for the rest of the fayre combined."

"Wow, that's amazing."

He holds out one of the cups of mulled wine for me. I reach out and take it, my fingers brushing against his as I do and reminding me that this isn't just about business, this is about us.

"So, our conversation earlier," I say. "Wow, that feels like so much longer ago."

"It really does," he agrees.

"I'd really appreciate it if we could go on another date. And I promise to try not to pull away if you want to kiss me again after it."

"What if I wanted to kiss you again during it?" he asks, his eyes sparkling with something akin to mischief.

My mouth goes dry. "I promise to try not to run away then either," I whisper, my gaze slipping to his lips while I try not to fixate too much on what it will feel like to kiss him.

He reaches out and takes the mulled wine cup back from me, placing it down on the counter along with his own. He steps closer, and all I can focus on is his proximity and the heat radiating off him. "What if I kissed you now?"

I look up and meet his gaze. "Then I definitely won't run away."

He leans in as my eyes flutter closed. It isn't until his lips meet mine that I fully register what's happening, and how right it feels for this to be happening. Everything fades away, there are no more aching muscles, there's no more tiredness or awareness that there's still more work to be done, all that remains is the way it feels to be kissing him.

I wrap my arms around his neck and pull him closer still, deepening the kiss and allowing myself to get even more lost in it.

And in that moment, I'm certain that this isn't going to be anything like the relationship I had with Mickey. It's going to be so much more. In a lot of ways that's scary, but in most, it just feels right.

We break apart, both of us smiling as we do. "So I guess that's a yes to a second date?" I murmur.

"A definite yes," he responds, leaning his forehead against mine.

Warmth fills me, not unlike if I'd drunk the mulled wine he brought, but so much better at the same time.

# Chapter 16

Edward

Cool air rises from the ice, only adding to the atmosphere around us. I'm not sure what I expected when I suggested to Rowen that we went ice skating, but somehow this is better than anything in my head.

"I'm going to warn you now that I haven't skated since I was nine," she says.

"Wouldn't it have been better to mention that before you had skates on?" I ask, trying to keep my bemusement out of my voice.

"Maybe I was worried that I wouldn't be able to find a way to hold onto your arm the whole date otherwise." I'm not sure if she's merely teasing, or if there's some truth in her words, but I don't suppose it matters.

"Well, if you're really bad at it, then we can do one lap of the ice so we've said we've done it, and then we can go inside, find a nice booth at the bar and drink hot chocolate while we talk about what terrible ice skaters we are," I suggest.

"I like the sound of that," she admits. "Help me onto the ice?" She eyes the rink warily.

I hold out my hand and she takes it in her own, though it's clear I didn't fully think this through as the gloves we're wearing don't allow us to properly hold hands.

"Want me to talk you through it?" I ask.

She shakes her head. "I think I've got it." She steps onto the ice, and I can see the moment her memory kicks in and she realises that she remembers what she's doing. Rowen lets go of my hand and glides out onto the ice. Her movements are choppy, but she's certainly not about to fall over.

I push away from the wall to join her, misjudging the force I need drastically. I cry out as I lose my balance and collapse to the floor, hitting my tailbone hard and wincing.

"Edward!" She glides back to me with surprising speed. "Are you okay?" Despite her concern, there's also a hint of amusement in her voice.

"My pride is wounded more than my body," I quip, then wince as I move and my body decides to try and prove me wrong.

She smothers a laugh. "Can you get up or do you need help?"

"I've got it." I struggle to my feet, huffing and puffing with every movement. "This was a terrible idea for a first date."

"Then it's a good job it's our second," she replies. "Come on, let's go get some hot chocolate instead."

"Are you sure? I promised ice skating?"

"True, but if you're going to hurt yourself, then it's not worth it. And like you said, we can find a nice corner booth and sit close together." She leans into me, the scent of her perfume filling my senses, it's not unlike the smells from the bakery in a lot of ways, though I'm sure if I said as much, she'd do her best to inform me of all the minute differences between the two of them. "That does sound nice."

"It does," I agree.

"You know what sounds even nicer?" she asks, a slightly teasing note in her voice.

"Mmm?"

"Once we've had our hot chocolate, perhaps we could go back to the bakery and I could make you one of my own and we can compare."

I raise an eyebrow. "You know what that sounds like, right?"

She skates backwards and cocks her head to the side, a slight smile lifting at the corners of her lips. "Yes."

I have to admit that isn't the answer I expect. "Right."

"Unless you don't want to. I promise I'm not ex-pecting anything more than a drink," she says quickly. "It's just that I've been around people so much in the past week that the idea of a quiet drink with you sounds really good."

"It does," I agree. "But you run a bakery, aren't you used to being around people?"

"I normally don't work front of house, it's just for events that I do."

"That makes so much sense."

"Are you trying to tell me that I'm not a people person?" she asks.

"Yes."

She lets out an amused laugh. "I don't think I'm that bad, but point taken. Shall we?" She gestures towards the area where we can take our skates off and hand them back to the hiring desk. I hope no one judges us for giving up so quickly, but if they saw my fall, then there's a chance they won't blame us for it.

"I'll be just a moment," I promise, mostly because I fear that the moment I move, I'm going to regret it. I'm certainly going to be feeling the fall for days to come.

She nods and heads back onto solid ground.

I take a deep breath and follow, wincing as I do. By the time I'm sitting down, Rowen has already taken her skates back and retrieved her bag from the lockers.

"Here," she says, handing me a blister pack of painkillers.

"You just carry these around with you?"

"I do. Though if you'll let me, I know a spell that'll do the trick at least twice as fast, and twice as strong."

"Please, be my guest."

She pulls out her wand and clears her throat before tapping it three times against my knee. She doesn't say the words out loud, which isn't surprising, most witches and warlocks don't need to for simple spells.

The pain instantly vanishes. "You're going to have to teach me that one," I say.

"If you want me to, but that's only the tip of the iceberg of what I know."

"Now I'm intrigued."

She chuckles. "I'm a witch who infuses baking with magical emotions, do you really think a painkiller spell is the best of my abilities?"

"Huh, I never thought about how you were actually doing the emotion thing," I admit. But now that I think about it, the magic needed is going to be impressive. I don't imagine just anyone could pull it off.

I lean down and tug off my ice skates, glad I thought to wear new socks tonight and not some of my faded old ones. That wouldn't be a good impression to give her.

"If we skip the hot chocolate here, and go straight back to the bakery, I can show you."

"I'd like that." And not just because it means that I get to spend more alone time with her, though that is admittedly still part of the decision.

She holds out her hand to help me stand. We end up standing closer together than necessary, but I seize my chance to steal a kiss, knowing that she'll happily reciprocate.

I brush her hair away from her cheek and lean down, capturing her lips with mine and kissing her deeply. I don't know how I'm so sure about her, but right now, I don't care. I can tell that my future is with Rowen.

CHAPTER 17

ROWEN

Oakley's soft singing comes from her cupcake workroom, while Hazel unloads a tray of macaron shells on her station, and I ice the decorations onto a new set of gingerbread men. The Christmas orders have been coming in thick and fast ever since the fayre ended, and while it's great for the bakery, and for our profits, it means that we're having to work even harder than normal to make sure they're all fulfilled. It's times like this that I'm glad we pulled out Granny's old kitchen and replaced it with one that's big enough for us all to work.

Though if Ash and Clover were also in the room, it might be a bit of a squeeze, but I suspect if that ever has to happen, we'll simply take shifts.

The urge to yawn overtakes me, and I set down my piping bag so I can step back and cover my mouth with my arm.

"Late night?" Oakley asks as she enters the room.

"I was in bed by nine," I murmur.

"Which is a clever way of saying that Edward was over last night," Hazel says.

"Mmhmm." Oakley grins. "Is he coming to Christmas Eve dinner?"

"I haven't asked him," I admit.

"You should. Antonio and Justin are coming," Hazel says.

"Yes, but you've both been dating them for months, I can barely claim that I've been dating Edward for weeks," I point out.

"True, but you're the kind of person who doesn't date unless it's serious," Hazel points out. "Which means that you see this going somewhere."

I let out a loud sigh. "I don't know where it's going." Though I suppose there's truth in what she's saying. One of the reasons I didn't date much between Mickey and Edward is because I never met anyone who I thought was worth the time.

"Invite him," Oakley says firmly. "Oh, and I think Clover wants to talk to you."

I frown. "Is everything all right?"

"I'm not her keeper, ask her yourself," she responds, gesturing to the shop door.

"That's fair," I murmur, heading through the door and into the shop.

"Oh, hey Rowen," Clover says as I step through.

"Oak said you wanted to talk."

She lets out a loud sigh. "Of course she did."

"I can go away if you want."

"No, she's right, I do." She shifts from side to side. "So you know how you said that Ash was going to join the bakery?"

"Mmhmm. Do you not want him to?" I have to admit, that's surprising, I always thought they got on well, especially when the two of them worked for weeks at Willow's coffee shop with one another.

"Of course I do, it'd be great to have Ash here."

"Okay, so what is it? Clo? Is everything all right?"

She sighs. "This is harder than I thought it would be."

"You're going to have to tell me what *this* is," I point out. "I can't do anything about it if you don't."

"I know, I'm just dealing with trying to figure out the best way to say it." She takes a deep breath.

I lean against the side and resist the urge to cross my arms, not wanting her to feel like I'm disapproving of whatever is going on in her head, even if I don't fully understand what's going on here.

"I want to do more than just work out the front," she blurts.

"Okay," I respond slowly. "I mean, you already do. You make the baklava."

"That's not what I mean," she murmurs. "I guess I've just been talking to Willow, and she thinks this is a good idea, and I haven't been able to get it out of my head."

"You still haven't told me what *this* is." And I'm starting to get worried, I don't think I've ever seen

Clover like this before, it's unlike her not to have a clear idea of anything.

"I want to write a recipe book."

"Oh."

"Oh? That's not a good *oh*, is it?"

"I'm just surprised," I promise. "But if it's what you want to do, then I think it's a good idea."

She stares at me. "You do?"

"Of course. Why wouldn't I?"

"I'm not sure. I'd want to do it under the Broomstick Bakery name."

"Which makes sense, and will benefit the bakery," I point out. "I'm still not sure which part of this you thought I wouldn't like."

"Sometimes it feels like your business plans are so rigid that they don't leave a lot of room for things like this."

"Oh, I hadn't realised. I'm sorry, and I'll try to do better." I don't want any of my siblings to feel like they can't have a say in how things are run. In fact, the opposite is true. "Maybe we should change how we run meetings. Sorry, that's something to focus on for another time. But seriously, if you want to write a recipe book, then I think it's a good idea."

She relaxes, seeming better than she has in a few weeks. "Thanks, Rowen. I've actually kind of been working on it already."

I let out an amused laugh. "Why am I not surprised?"

"Because you're not the only workaholic in the family," she quips.

"Speaking of, I need to go tidy my workspace. Edward's coming over in about ten minutes and I promised him dinner, I can't do that if I'm still decorating gingerbread men."

Clover stares at me. "You're leaving work unfinished so you can go on a date?"

"Yes? Is that bad? Should I not do it? I can message him and postpone."

"Don't you even dare," she warns. "It's a great thing. But don't worry about tidying up, I can do that for you."

"Are you sure?"

She nods. "Absolutely. Go."

"Thanks." I smile and head back into the kitchen, saying a quick goodnight to both Hazel and Oakley and telling them to send Edward up when he arrives.

There's a small part of me that wants to hurry back into the kitchen and finish the work I'm part way through, but I know that it can wait, especially when there's other time to finish it, and other parts of my life to enjoy.

I change out of my work times and am heading towards the small kitchen boasted by my flat when there's a knock on the door.

"Come in," I call, knowing that there's only one person it can possibly be. Especially since my sisters don't knock.

The door opens and Edward steps inside.

"Hey." I head over and go up on my toes to give him a kiss. "I haven't started cooking yet."

"You don't have to if you don't want," he says. "We can go out or order takeaway..."

I shake my head. "I want to."

"Good, because I don't really want to leave." He pulls his tie loose and strips it off, shrugging off his suit jacket soon after.

"I like the idea of staying in too," I say as I start to get the ingredients ready. "But speaking of food, I have a question."

"What is it?"

"So, my family has this big Christmas Eve dinner every year, it's not super fancy, but everyone goes, and I wanted to know if you wanted to come." I don't even realise I'm going to ask him until the words are out of my mouth.

"I'd love to," he responds.

"Are you sure? I know you've met my siblings, but this'll mean my parents and grandparents too."

"Are *you* sure that you want me there?" he asks.

"Yes."

"Then I want to be there." He reaches out and pulls me into his arms.

"Great, then it's a date."

"I'll give it a recurring slot in my diary," he responds.

And while such a strong promise of the future should scare me, it doesn't. Because when I'm with Edward, I feel like I can see a long way ahead, and I'm looking forward to discovering every minute of it.

***

Thank you for reading *The Gingerbread Witch*, I hope you enjoyed it! If you want to continue the series with the final book, you can with *The Baklava Witch*.

AUTHOR NOTE

Thank you for reading *The Gingerbread Witch*, I hope you enjoyed it!

Ever since Broomstick Bakery sprang to mind in my head, I knew that there would need to be a Christmas story, and Rowen seemed the perfect choice partly because she's so serious and it would allow me to properly explore another side of her. The sibling bond throughout the series is an important part of the stories and the dynamic, and this book explored one of the dynamics that I'm very familiar with - a much older sister with the youngest brother. While the age gap between me and my youngest brother is actually slightly bigger than the ten years between Rowen and Ash, I found myself channelling a lot of how I feel about my brother through Rowen's eyes (Rowen is a year younger than I am, so it was an easy leap to make!)

If you've been reading the rest of the *Broomstick Bakery* series, then you'll know that each of the siblings has had a story of their own - Oakley in (book 1), Hazel in (book 2), Ash in (a side story set between books 2 & 3), and the series will end with Clover in (book 4). It's going to be sad to say goodbye to the witches of Broomstick Bakery, but they'll continue to appear as side characters in Willow and Azíl's series, .

If you want to keep up to date with new releases and other news, you can join my or .

Stay safe & happy reading!

- Laura

Also By Laura Greenwood

Signed Paperback & Merchandise:

You can find signed paperbacks, hardcovers, and merchandise based on my series (including stickers, magnets, face masks, and more!) via my website.

Series List:

* denotes a completed series

The Obscure World

A paranormal & urban fantasy world where supernaturals live out in the open alongside humans. Each series can be read on its own, but there are cameos from past characters and mentions of previous events.

Cauldron Coffee Shop - Broomstick Bakery - Obscure Academy - The Shifter Season - Stonerest Academy -

<u>Harker Academy</u> - <u>Ashryn Barker</u>* - <u>Grimalkin Academy</u>* - <u>City Of Blood</u>* - <u>Grimalkin Vampires</u>* - <u>Supernatural Retrieval Agency</u>* - <u>The Black Fan</u>* - <u>Sabre Woods Academy</u>* - <u>Scythe Grove Academy</u>*

The Forgotten Gods World

A fantasy romance world based on Egyptian mythology. Each series can be read on its own, but there are cameos from past characters and mentions of previous events.

<u>Forgotten Gods</u> - <u>The Queen of Gods</u>* - <u>Forgotten Gods: Origins</u>*

The Egyptian Empire

A modern fantasy world set in an alternative timeline where the Egyptian Empire never fell.

<u>The Apprentice Of Anubis</u>

The Paranormal Council Universe

A paranormal romance & urban fantasy world where paranormals are hidden away from the human world, and are in search of their fated mates. Each series can be read on its own, but there are cameos from past characters and mentions of previous events.

The Paranormal Council Series* - The Fae Queens* - Paranormal Criminal Investigations* - The Necromancer Council* - Return Of The Fae*

Other Series

Purple Oasis (with Arizona Tape) - Grimm Academy - Beyond The Curse* - Untold Tales* - The Dragon Duels* - Speed Dating With The Denizens Of The Underworld (shared world) - Seven Wardens* (with Skye MacKinnon) - Tales Of Clan Robbins (co-written with L.A. Boruff) - Firehouse Witches* (with Lacey Carter Andersen & L.A. Boruff) - Valentine Pride* (with Lainie Anderson) - Magic and Metaphysics Academy* (with Lainie Anderson)

Twin Souls Universe

A paranormal romance & urban fantasy world co-written with Arizona Tape. Each series can be read on its own, but there are cameos from past characters and mentions of previous events.

Amethyst's Wand Shop Mysteries - Twin Souls* - The Vampire Detective*

About Laura Greenwood

Laura is a USA Today Bestselling Author of paranormal, fantasy, urban fantasy, and contemporary romance. When she's not writing, she drinks a lot of tea, tries to resist French macarons, and works towards a diploma in Egyptology. She lives in the UK, where most of her books are set. Laura specialises in quick reads, whether you're looking for a swoonworthy romance for the bath, or an action-packed adventure for your latest journey, you'll find the perfect match amongst her books!

Follow Laura Greenwood

Website: www.authorlauragreenwood.co.uk

Mailing List: https://www.authorlauragreenwood.co.uk/p/book-sign-up.html

Facebook Group: http://facebook.com/groups/theparanormalcouncil

Facebook Page: http://facebook.com/authorlauragreenwood

Bookbub: www.bookbub.com/authors/laura-greenwood